# Simon's Run and Other Adventures

by

## Stuart de Jong

I0629425

SADD Writings Publisher LLC

Cover art by Deborah de Jong

ISBN 979-8-9902944-1-7 (paperback)
ISBN 979-8-9902944-0-0 (ebook)

Published by SADD Writings Publisher LLC
https://SaddWritings.com

## Acknowledgements

Thank you to my wife Debbie for supporting all of my endeavors, proofreading early versions of my story, and designing and illustrating the book cover. Also, thank you to my beta-readers, Peter de Jong and Susan Appelbaum, for their feedback and suggestions.

# Table of Contents

# PROLOGUE

Nurse Jody Hansen was only one month out of nursing school, but she was currently the only nurse manning the maternity ward. Two nurses had called in sick at the last minute, and it would be another hour before their replacements arrived. They had to commute into Manhattan from New Jersey. She assumed their illnesses were related to the holiday season; she took her responsibilities more seriously. In the meantime, she was feeling quite harried.

"Dr. Evans, Dr. Evans," Jody called out to the doctor walking away from her down the hall.

"What is it, Nurse?" Dr. Evans impatiently replied.

"It's the Zane baby, Simon, in room eight. This is the third time in the last couple of hours that he's had trouble breathing. It's like he's choking," Nurse Jody reported.

"You are going to have to deal with this on your own. My priority is the Streisand kid in room one. When he starts to have trouble breathing, just spank him on the bottom. If that doesn't do the trick, hold him upside down by his ankles and slap his feet, got it?" Dr. Evans directed.

"Yes, Doctor," Nurse Jody dutifully replied.

"Good!" Dr. Evans then set off down the hall to attend to his much more important patient. After taking a few steps, he suddenly remembered something else that was important to him and turned around. Nurse Jody was now facing away from him, and he could see what a great figure she had. She couldn't have been more than nineteen years old and was a stunner. "Oh, Jody?" he called back.

Nurse Jody slowly turned around, feeling a little flush. Hearing Dr. "Ted" Evans refer to her as just Jody made her heart flutter. "Yes, Dr. Evans?" Jody said shyly.

"When your shift is over at ten tonight, why don't you come by my office. We can discuss patient treatment techniques, among other things. What do you say?" Dr. Evans said smoothly.

"Okayyy..." Nurse Jody tried to play it cool but was beaming inside. Dr. Evans was brilliant and handsome and had been flirting with her since she arrived. When she told her mom that Dr. Evans seemed interested in her, her mom was elated. A rich doctor was interested in her daughter; this was her dream come true. As Dr. Evans disappeared into room one, she found herself daydreaming about dinner parties and picket fences. She wouldn't blow her "date" with Dr. Evans tonight.

A few moments later she was rudely knocked out of her reverie, hearing Simon's mother calling her from room eight. "God, what now?" she whispered to herself. "How can I help you, Mrs. Zane?" she asked in her most professional voice.

"Simon, Simon, he's having trouble breathing. Please help," Mrs. Zane said.

Nurse Jody quickly grabbed the baby by the ankles and smacked him hard on his feet two times, not bothering to try the spanking first. As Dr. Evans predicted, this worked wonderfully and Simon's breathing quickly returned to normal, though after a few breaths, he started screaming.

"You hurt him!" Mrs. Zane said accusingly.

"I administered the treatment prescribed by Dr. Evans. He is brilliant and there is no need to question his treatments. Your baby can breathe again," she scolded Mrs. Zane.

With that, Nurse Jody left the room and closed the door behind her. That screaming baby and ungrateful mother were really starting to annoy her. They were trouble. She walked to the nurses' station, sat down, and took a few deep breaths. She started imagining her new life with Ted, living in a nice house with a picket fence on Long Island. Nineteen sixty-seven would be her year.

# Humble Beginnings

"Teennn?"

"Yes, Simon, I want you to count to ten," the school counselor asked patiently.

"Ten!" I replied.

"No, Simon, I want you to count to ten."

"Ten!"

"You know, start at one, then two, and then count to ten," the counselor countered, trying to lead me to the answer.

"One, two, and ten!" I replied with an expression like I had just discovered the secret to nuclear fusion.

"What number comes after two?"

"Ten!" I replied triumphantly.

The counselor sighed and spent a brief moment looking at her notepad. "Okay, Simon, you are doing really well," she blandly stated. Then talking more slowly to me now than before, she continued, "Let's try something else. What day of the week is it?"

"Today," I stated.

"Yes, Simon, what day of the week is today?"

"Uuuuh, I don't know," I replied with a confused look on my face.

The counselor took a moment to write down more stuff on her notepad, then looked at me sympathetically. "I think I have all the information I need. Let's go get your mom in and talk things over. Does that sound good to you?"

Not waiting for my reply, she got up from the chair, opened the door, and asked my mother in. My mother sat down in the chair next to mine as the counselor made her way back behind her desk. It took a little effort because the room was very cramped, and the counselor was on the larger side.

"Now, Ms. Zane, let me start by saying you have a very sweet little child. I look forward to getting to know him better and working with him in the future."

My mother's expression changed from anxiousness to confusion. "My child is very sweet?"

"Yes, don't you think so?" the counselor replied.

Wanting to get directly to the matter at hand, my mother ignored the question and asked about the results of my test.

The counselor tightened her lips and cut straight to the chase. "Your son is mildly retarded," she then quickly continued, "but with the right tutoring, I think there is a chance he'll be able to have a fairly normal life as an adult. It's good to catch issues like this early so we can still have a chance to positively affect the outcome."

My mother was now incredulous. "Simon is not retarded!"

"No, Ms. Zane, he is mildly retarded, which is much different. As I said, there is still a chance we can get him to the point where he can hold down a job, though usually people with low IQs have menial jobs."

"What you are saying makes no sense at all. My son is very smart."

"Every parent thinks their child is smart," the counselor condescended. "My job is to make sure every child has an opportunity to be educated to the best of their ability, and to do that, we need to know what they are capable of learning. Simon is eight years old and cannot count to ten, which to me is concerning."

My mother quickly countered, "Of course he can count to ten, he just didn't want to."

"I'm not going to argue with you, Ms. Zane. I've been doing this for a long time, and as I said, my job is to do what is best for Simon. My findings will go into his permanent record, but we'll help him learn up to his capabilities and possibly reevaluate him a few years from now."

With that, the meeting was over. My mother constrained herself from arguing with the counselor further. After sitting there this whole time with a grin on my face, I asked my mom if we could go to Burger King. I was really hungry.

"How about you count to ten for the counselor, and then I'll take you to Burger King."

"Aaaahhhhhhaaaaahaaaaahhhhhhhaaaaaahhhhhhaa ahh!" I started screaming.

Alarmed, the counselor sternly told my mother that she was being cruel to me and would note it in her report.

Embarrassed by my sudden tantrum, she relented and told me, "Fine, we'll go to Burger King!"

I immediately stopped screaming and went back to grinning. Manipulating adults was fun.

Burger King was my favorite restaurant. I ate my ketchup-drenched fries slowly to make them last, but the Whopper was too good, so I couldn't help but eat it quickly. My bliss was rudely interrupted by my mother when she told me that I would have to go back to the counselor's office the next day to count to ten and recite the days of the week.

"I can't," I replied simply.

"Why not?" she asked.

"Because today is Friday and there is no school on Saturday."

"So, you do know the days of the week!" my mother said accusingly.

"Duh!"

"Why didn't you cooperate with the counselor? You being retarded is now part of your permanent record."

"Partially retarded," I corrected her.

"I give up," my mother sighed, resigned to our fate.

After a few moments of silence, I finished my last fry. I thought about asking for another order but decided not to. At some point, I'd push my mom too far and get a beating. It's always a fine line to push her right up to that point but not over. It's an art, really.

"It's going to be very hard for you to get a good job with this on your permanent record," my mother finally continued.

"Don't need a job, I have twenty-two dollars that Great Grandpa gave me last time we went to visit him."

Looking a little confused, she said, "Wait, Grandpa gave you fifty dollars in silver half dollars, not twenty-two."

"That's how much I have left. I use it when I need something at the stationery store." The stationery store was in downtown Demarest, and what I really meant was that I used it to buy candy there.

My mother knew this, so questions followed, "Wait, you're using your silver half dollars to buy candy? Those were meant for you to save. Maybe you are retarded."

"Maybe I'll start screaming again," I threatened.

After sitting there for a few more moments in silence, I finished my meal and asked if I could get another order of fries.

# THE PEA INCIDENT

"Finish those peas!" Stepbad boomed.

"There are too many," Sister complained.

"Before you leave this table, you will finish those ten peas. I counted them out myself, and we agreed you would eat that many."

With tears streaming down her cheeks, Sister whimpered, "No, I didn't!"

This was a battle of attrition, but ultimately, Stepbad would win. He had no trouble employing torture in the form of misery infusion to get his way. A pre-teen girl is not always rational and can be very stubborn, but a largish, drunkard, middle-aged tyrant will either get his way or make you pay for it later. After a short standoff, Sister ate the peas and ran from the table. A few seconds later, a door slammed upstairs.

My mother just sat there resigned, and I just went back to eating, being used to this type of chaos, and I was hungry. My twin cousins happened to be visiting us that day, so they were at the table with us. Nora just looked down with a sad expression and picked at her food. Will was looking up, wild-eyed and moving his eyes back and forth like a wired cat. He took my cue and shortly went back to eating. Nora and Will weren't strangers to household chaos, so they weathered the storm like pros.

Stepbad kept eating, but also furiously complained to his audience that Sister needed to show more respect and blamed Mom for not backing him up. Mom had already left the table to move things around the kitchen and start cleaning up. I just tuned everything out and kept eating, head down, until all the food was gone. Not that I wasn't stressed; I was very stressed, but eating made me feel better. I knew this would be a bad night, but luckily, I had a bottle of NyQuil up in my room to help me sleep through the nightly storm.

In the hour after dinner, things were pretty quiet. Stepbad retreated to the basement to do whatever it was he did down there. It also happened to be where he stored his cases of canned Budweiser. Nora, Will, Sister, and I just hung out playing games until my aunt came and picked the cousins up. Stepbad did make an appearance before they left; however, it was only to drunkenly shout about some nonsense. My aunt just said, "Oh my god. What's the matter with you?" He replied about something, and then they all left. I went to my room, took my shot of NyQuil, and thankfully slept through that night's turmoil.

Morning was the best time. I was always up first, and the house was quiet. I could gather my things, make my breakfast, and be out of there just as I started hearing the sounds of Stepbad getting ready for work. I was out the door a little after 7:00 AM. It was mostly a quiet walk to school, more so in the winter when it was cold and there was snow on the ground. The walk to and from school was a time of peace.

For the first hour after I arrived, I hit the weight room. The wrestling team lifted weights before school started in the morning and practiced after school. It wasn't really a weight room, more like sets of well-used weights and equipment stuffed into the backend of the stage overlooking the school gym. It wasn't fancy, but it was still enough to accomplish what we needed. After getting through the fixed routine, it was down to the basement locker room for showers and back up to start classes. Fortunately, Bruce wasn't there to pee on our legs while showering this morning. I'm sure it was just Bruce's way of expressing himself and having a little fun. There were much worse things that happened in the locker room than getting peed on in the shower. Your best bet was to just keep your head down and let someone else be the victim. This was good advice, both inside and outside the locker room in high school.

I wasn't into sports or very good at them, but participating in sports meant less time at home. It also meant I could hang out with other kids, since outside of school, I was mostly alone. Given the situation at home, I was too embarrassed to ever invite anybody over, so I didn't have any close friends; the ones I had when I was younger had mostly moved away. By midday I was starving and ready for lunch. It was fun hanging out with the other kids in the lunchroom, trading wisecracks; it was the best period of the day.

My days normally went smoothly. There was the usual high school drama and tension in the hallways, but I kept out of it, so I wasn't usually bothered by anybody. I got good grades without having to work very hard, which probably would have surprised my grammar school counselor. Not having to work too hard in school to do well came back to bite me later in college when this same work ethic resulted in very bad grades.

The worst part of the day was after-school wrestling practice. It started with a long run, then moved to sprints, and then to actual wrestling practice. I did it because I had to do something other than just go home, but I didn't enjoy it. When I had to fight at meets, I got nervous to the point of nausea. Much of what determined who would win a match at the JV level came down to conditioning. I was in excellent shape and could thankfully wrestle in the hundred-pound weight class without having to forgo all food before the match, but by the time it was my turn to wrestle, the nervousness and stress had completely drained me of all energy. My match was always first or second, and I usually lost pretty quickly. Right after my match was over, the stress and nausea immediately abated, allowing me to relax and enjoy the rest of the matches as just a spectator. I liked to win but didn't really care if I lost, unlike some of the other guys, where losing could ruin their day.

# RUNNING

Junior year, I decided that, to make wrestling practices less excruciating at the start of the season, I had to get in really good shape beforehand. The solution was to move the pain of getting into shape up a few months, by joining the cross-country team.

Compared to wrestling or running track, cross-country wasn't so bad. You could be very competitive if you were a top runner and wanted to be, but there was also a place for the other boys and girls who were slower and just wanted to run. It was pretty laid-back and didn't involve any combat. Being average at cross-country didn't require any special skills, you just had to put on a pair of sneakers and run. I usually finished towards the middle or back of the pack but had a really fast kick at the finish line, so I was actually the best of the mediocre.

Our school did have two very good runners, one on the boys' team and one on the girls' team. Mike was good enough to always be at the front of the pack and also happened to sit at the same table as me during study hall. He wasn't the type to brag about his accomplishments, but I always made sure he knew that even though he was much faster than me on race day, unlike him, I had run the New York City Marathon and finished in under three hours. You could brag about fake accomplishments just as easily as real ones. The fake ones might even be better. Nobody believed me anyway; it just wasn't plausible.

Running cross-country before wrestling season worked as planned. During the hard practices in the run-up to the start of the season, I would breeze right through the running and sprinting portions of practice. It wasn't necessarily fun, but being able to get through practice without experiencing pain and exhaustion made it much more pleasant. In addition to improving my overall wrestling practice experience, I won some matches. I won zero matches in my freshman and sophomore years, but in my junior year, I actually won a few.

In addition, I beat up (sort of) another wrestler on the team named Jordan. He liked to pick on me, so me beating him up really delighted the other members of the team. Picking on someone and then having the tables turned on you while everyone was watching was one of the best ways to make yourself a hazing target. The worst things that can happen to you in a locker room, worse than getting peed on in the shower, now happened to Jordan. For example, getting thrown out the door naked in the middle of winter or getting stuffed in a locker and forgotten about were worse than getting peed on. Unsurprisingly, Jordan didn't rejoin the team Senior year, but then again, I didn't either.

While I was never going to be a great or even a good wrestler, I did continue to run. I ran on the track team, though mostly didn't compete. Unlike cross-country, the coaches just ignored me because I wasn't going to win any trophies. After school ended for the year, I continued to

14

go out on runs around my neighborhood. I wasn't one of those runners who felt a high from running, but sometimes I could forget where I was and just run and daydream and rack up the miles in a meditative state. There were other benefits too, like fueling up mid-run on a whopper and fries. It was especially good on the weekend when I needed to get out of the house and away from Stepbad.

# THE GREAT RUN

I just decided to keep going. After running the three miles to the entrance of Palisades Park, I felt this urge to just keep going and not go back home, so I made my way back up to Route 9W and headed North. After thirty minutes of running, I was hot and sweaty and out of water, but I kept going anyway. It's not the best place to run with all the cars whizzing by, and some of them seemed to swerve over into the shoulder just to screw with me; there are a lot of assholes in New Jersey. A few cars slowed down so the occupants could shout, "get the fuck off the road," and many other clever comments. At this point, I was too tired and thirsty to care; the whole endeavor was senseless; I didn't even like running that much.

After a while, I started to lose myself in daydreams. I was the captain of a battleship shooting lasers down on Earth; fighting the aliens and giving orders. Just as I was preparing for the battle against the opposing force, I felt a blast of air from a car whizzing by, knocking me back to reality, but thankfully I'd made lots of headway while my head was off in the clouds.

It had been almost an hour and a half before I turned off Route 9W and made my way onto more local streets. I came up alongside a marina where I sneaked around to the side of a building to find a faucet. I got down onto the ground and just let the cold water pour over my head for several minutes. The cool water felt great running over my head and down my shirt, cooling my skin. It smelled of the ocean, with that rotting mollusk smell mixed with a little gasoline. The sun was still beating down on me, and I was sticky and chafing. After getting my fill of water and refilling my water bottle, I continued my trek north. At this location, the Tappan Zee Bridge was fully in view, so I made it my goal to just get to the bridge. It only took me another twenty minutes to get there, but another ten after that to find an entrance to the bridge walkway, which was up the highway and away from the river. I had been running for around two hours and my legs and back hurt, and my feet were starting to blister, but it was much cooler by the water, and I had always wanted to walk across the George Washington Bridge. This wasn't that bridge, but it was the bridge I was on at that moment, so I continued on to New York.

It was much cooler on the bridge, but the wind was blowing me sideways, making it hard to stay balanced on my chewed-up feet. My choices were to try and change my stride to a jog walk (I wouldn't call what I was doing running anymore) or try to ignore the pain from the blisters. The problem was, when I changed my stride, my back started to hurt more. The whole adventure was starting to seem more foolish by the minute, but I'd set my goal to get across the bridge, so couldn't stop now. The bridge is only three miles long, but it took me a little over an hour to get to the New York side. After crossing, I couldn't go on anymore and couldn't go back either. I found a little forested area close to some train tracks that parallel the river and lay down, exhausted.

I woke up confused, forgetting where I was. After a few seconds, I snapped out of it and remembered lying down in the grass to get a short rest. It was nice down there, the river was calm, and the city lights reflected off the water to give the whole area a light glow. I was pretty cold though, and only wearing the shorts and tee shirt I had on from the day before. My back ached with soreness while sitting up; my muscles were completely stiffened. As I pushed myself back up on my feet, I felt the sharp pain from those blisters I had blissfully forgotten about. My feet were also soaked since I hadn't had the foresight to remove my socks and shoes before passing out. I started to do that, and the smell almost overpowered me. The situation wasn't good, but at least without my shoes on I could walk across the soft grass to find a tree to water. With that mission accomplished, I gave my feet an hour to dry out while I napped some more and then got myself going again on my journey.

It was 4:30 AM when I moved on out, and the early commuters were already filling the roads. I passed by a closed pizza shop, which was just as well since I hadn't brought any money with me anyway; my original plan was to run three miles to the Palisades and back home. I did, however, spot a pizza box on a bench beside the shop and scored three slices of plain pizza that were inside. It smelled alright and I hadn't eaten for at least a day, so I quickly ate all three slices. A block later, I saw a woman throw a Dunkin' Donuts bag into the garbage, and on a hunch, I went in to find an almost whole jelly donut just sitting there waiting for me to eat it. After the pizza and donut, I had a full belly and a full bottle of water. It was cool out and I was feeling pretty good, so I started my slow jog south towards Manhattan on Broadway.

I jogged for another two hours before getting to Yonkers. I'd been able to fill some of that time with more daydreams about commanding spaceships, but my legs couldn't go much further. At this rate, it would take me days to get back home. I headed a block down a side street to find a place to sit and rest and maybe find some more leftover food. I dozed off for I don't know how long, but was rudely brought back to the present when I felt a hand clutching my shoulder. It was not a friendly grip, and my breath immediately started to get heavy. The butterflies started flying, I knew I was in trouble. Then a man with red curly hair and bright blue eyes got right in my face and said he was going to kill me. He slapped me upside the head to make the point clearer. I was too scared to talk and couldn't run away because the guy behind me was pressing down on both my shoulders. Red was still in my face, smiling now.

He had horrible breath which smelled like cigarettes and beer, and mixed with my fear, was making me nauseous. I think he saw me curl my nose, so he opened his mouth wide and blew hot stinky air right into my face. I couldn't help but choke a little on the smell. "Now you gone hurt my feelin's," he said, before pulling me off the bench and tossing me on the ground. I felt a sharp pain in my lower back from the point of his shoe as he kicked me a couple of times. The pain and fear together were almost too much, and I felt like I was going to puke. "What are you, some kind of pussy? Hey, Shane, this faggot won't even fight back," he spat out. Shane and Red rolled me on my stomach and went through my pockets. They found them empty, which I think really pissed them off. They started beating me with their fists in my mid-section, as I curled up into fetal position. Now that I'd numbed a little, it wasn't so bad, so I just waited for them to tire out and hoped they wouldn't start stomping me on the head.

Suddenly, they stopped and ran away. I looked up a minute later to see a cop car parked right beside me. "Kid, you alright?" he asked me.

It seemed obvious that I was not, but I told him that I was okay anyway.

"I'm Officer O'Brian, let me help you up." After he got me on my feet and looked me over, he offered me a ride home, probably thinking I was a local. I declined and said I'd just walk back to the main road and call my mom from the public telephone. He didn't go away that easily, but luckily, he got a call on his radio and had somewhere more important to be. I told him I was fine one more time, smiled, and started walking back to Broadway. He didn't look convinced but got in his car, turned on the siren, and drove away.

I did go back to Broadway, but I didn't call my mom; instead, I cried for a few minutes. There was no way I was going to be stopped by my bruised ribs and spirit. Even after the beatdown, I'd still rather be there than home, I just had to be smarter and more aware of my surroundings. I tried to sit so I could recover a little, but then I started stiffening up, and the aches got worse. I got up and started walking with a slight limp on my right leg where one of those assholes kicked me. As I walked, I imagined myself a normal person, just out, going where I needed to be, like all these other people on the street and in their cars.

A few more hours went by before I arrived at The Cloisters Museum. It's surrounded by a big park, where I smelled food cooking, which reminded me that I was starving to death. I walked towards the smell and reached an open grassy area where there were crowds of people, mostly Hispanic. There was music playing and women and girls dressed up in colorful dresses, while the men wore jeans and tee shirts. Normally, I'd be too shy to crash a party, but on the side of the field were tables full of food, and I was almost delirious with hunger. I decided to play it cool and just walked over like I was supposed to be there. I loaded up an oversized paper plate with rice and beans and thinly sliced barbecued meat. I also added some tomato salsa and a side that looked like fried sliced bananas.

I found a spot a little away from the crowds under a tree and started eating. I was thinking I had gotten away with it when a teenage kid, probably around my age, walked over to me. "I don't remember inviting any gringos to my party," he said. I'd never been good with confrontation, so all I could say was, "This is your party?" He stared at me for a few more seconds with brown squinted eyes. He had honey-colored skin that was slightly pimpled and a smallish forehead. His hair was dark, almost black, and he was short like me. He looked sweaty, like he'd been running around in the dirt or playing ball. I didn't think I was in for another beating.

After a few more seconds of giving me his best impersonation of a tough guy, a smile broke out on his face. "Hey, I'm just kidding with you," he said. I felt some relief and told him I was just hungry and ... He interrupted me and said, "Don't worry about it, there is plenty of food." He plopped down, right next to me, and started talking. "My sister made those plantains; do you like them?" I looked a little confused, so he pointed to the banana-like things on my plate and repeated the word 'plantains' really slowly, like he was talking to a simpleton.

"Oh, I didn't know what they were called, I just thought somebody fried up bananas," I said.

"They are basically the same thing. Yo, what's your name?"

"I'm Simon, from New Jersey," I answered.

"I'm Jose, from the Bronx. Why you here if you from Jersey?"

"Yesterday, I went out for a run and decided I didn't want to go back home, so I just kept going, and now I'm here," I said.

That seemed to fascinate him. "Really, you ran all the way here from New Jersey. My Mom would kill me if I didn't come home. She'd think I was up to no good. Does your dad beat you or something?"

"No, I just needed to get away for a while. This morning, I found some leftovers to eat out on the street, so ..."

Jose interrupted, "No problem, eat as much as you want. I got you covered. Yo, come with me."

Jose led me across the field to another set of tables piled high with sweets. There were cookies topped with dabs of fruity jelly, cupcakes with multiple types of icing, fruit pies, pies I couldn't identify but smelled of cinnamon, ice cream, Jello, and it went on and on. I must have gone into a trance, since Jose had to slap me on the arm to bring me back to Earth. "Hey, Maria, this is my new friend Simon," Jose announced.

For some reason, I felt a little embarrassed when he called me his friend. I didn't have any friends back home. Sure, I had acquaintances and some kids I hung out with sometimes, but mostly I kept my own company. I'd been here for less than an hour and had already found a friend; maybe I had grown up in the wrong place. Hopefully, they wouldn't notice my awkwardness and nervous expression. They didn't seem to, so maybe they thought I was just overwhelmed with all of the dessert choices.

Maria followed with a heavy accent, "Well, Simon, it is nice to meet you."

"You have to try the cupcakes, Maria made the ones over here with chocolate icing," Jose said excitedly. "Simon ran all the way here from New Jersey and stopped by because he's hungry."

Maria looked me over. "You like cookies, Simon? Here, take some of these and a slice of pie too." She quickly loaded up my plate and continued, "I'm so glad you're here and made friends with my brother."

I tried to look away while she was making my plate so Jose wouldn't notice me staring at his sister. At that moment, she may have been the best-looking girl I had ever seen in my life. She had long black hair, dark skin, and eyes that I had to be careful not to stare into for very long, or I would get stuck. Her blouse was just low-cut enough so I could see the top of her breasts. I think I was starting to feel something strange, so I quickly thanked her, found some chairs over by the side, and dug into the sweets along with Jose, who also enthusiastically started eating.

Jose did notice and said, "You like my sister. Everybody does, but nobody goes near her because my cousin put out that he'll kill anybody who tries anything with her. He's loco and big, so most guys are scared to even talk to her."

I just continued munching on a cookie, embarrassed by where this conversation was going.

He continued, "I don't think you have anything to worry about, though."

I'm sure he didn't mean anything by it, but I felt insulted. I guess I was so non-threatening that even Jose's loco cousin would let me be friends with Maria. If I ever wound up in a room alone with her, I was sure I would just start hyperventilating anyway, so hooking up with Maria and getting killed by her cousin wasn't likely.

I managed to eat everything on my plate and started to feel jittery from all the sugar. I turned to Jose and said, "I probably need to get going pretty soon. I have to get back home today." It was mid-afternoon and I knew I wasn't getting all the way home before nightfall, but I wasn't used to socializing, so along with the sugar jitters

24

I was starting to feel very stressed and had to get out of there, even though I liked Jose.

"Alright man, are you doing this again?"

I didn't know but replied yes anyway.

"Just wait here for a second, I'll be right back." He walked back over to Maria's table, and I could see him writing something down. He ran back and handed me a scrap of paper with his name, address, and phone number written on it. "Maybe I can run with you, and then we can go back to my place and hang out," Jose said expectantly.

I looked down at the ground and said, "Ya, sure, I'll call you next time I run by." Jose smiled and I was off. I felt a little adrenaline push, so almost sprinted out of the park as I continued my run south to the George Washington Bridge. In no time, I was across the bridge and running the home stretch back to the start of my journey. I was so deep in thought that I barely noticed crossing the bridge. I'd need to pay more attention next time since it had always been something I wanted to do.

# THE HOME STRETCH

*"Commander, we have enemy contact," my first mate reported.*

*"Direct battle group A to maintain position behind the moon, but tell them to be ready to pounce on my command," I ordered.*

*As the three enemy ships approached, they positioned themselves to attack us broadside. I ordered my lieutenant to fire our laser canons as soon as they were in range. In the meantime, we randomly maneuvered through space to avoid being an easy target.*

*The enemy fired first, but before the missiles reached us, their ships came into range, and we fired everything we had. Their missiles did minimal damage but took out half our shields, so we wouldn't be so lucky the next time. Our two ships exchanged fire, causing equal damage. Just as I was starting to think we might not win this fight; the lead enemy ship exploded right down the middle and broke in half. Finally, our two battleships from behind the moon had made it to the party...*

As I was running along Henry Hudson Drive, a car got a little too close and woke me out of my daydream. I'd been running for over two hours since crossing the bridge and could see that I was finally approaching the marina. My back and feet were killing me, my bruised ribs ached, and my legs were very unsteady. Also, my intestines were bloated. In summary, I was a mess. For the first few miles after crossing the bridge, I had to stop multiple times because of stomach cramping. All that food I had eaten was looking for a new home.

Fortunately, I was at the Alpine Marina and the facilities were open. I did my business and then walked over to a more secluded beach area up away from the docks where I collapsed onto the sand. It was around 7:00 PM, but despite my tiredness, I didn't fall asleep for a long time. Notwithstanding starting the day with a beatdown, it had been one of the best days I'd had in a long time. I had a new friend and had talked to a pretty girl, or at least grunted at her with a stupid smile on my face. At least I didn't drool. I felt at peace; the air was cool and not too putrid. The waves were making a nice lapping sound by the shore. Eventually, it got dark, and the stars were starting to come out as I fell asleep.

I woke up to an old man in blue coveralls shaking my arm. He was skinny, so the coveralls looked like they were wearing him. The tag on the front said "Joe." His hair was thin and gray, and his skin was wrinkled and darkly tanned. I don't think he'd showered recently. I hadn't either, so I must have looked pretty bad to him too.

"There is no overnight sleeping at this park," Joe stated with authority.

"I was just taking a quick break, I didn't sleep here," I lied.

"Just wait here while I go report this. Don't move." Joe looked at me for a second more and then scurried off in slow motion.

When he was no longer in sight, I took off down the trail along the river, which then started switching back and forth up to the top of the cliffs. I'd probably got halfway up when the adrenaline from escaping the strong arm of the law hit me in the stomach. All of a sudden, all my choices from the last few days conspired against me and I had to run off the trail into the woods to relieve myself. Things got messy and all I had were leaves to try and clean myself. Now, in addition to all my other ailments, I had a bad rash.

Before I came into view of the trail again, I heard the static sound of a radio, so I sneaked a look from behind a tree and saw a cop walking up the trail. Joe really was serious about turning me in. All I could do at this point was sit down and wait it out. Unfortunately, the deposit I'd left in the woods had attracted swarms of flies. Between the flies, the mosquitos, and my squalid condition after three days of running and sleeping outside, I was feeling foul in mood and smell. I sat like that, getting eaten alive, for the next half hour.

Eventually, the cop came back down the trail, and he didn't look happy either. I was wondering if he'd got all the way to the top before giving up on finding me. The slight breeze was blowing away from me towards the trail and I noticed as he came around the corner he was grimacing and waving his hand across his face. Good, sharing is caring, it served him right for making me sit out there in my own stink. As soon as he was down the trail and out of range, I made my way back to the trail and high-tailed it up to the top, across the Palisades Parkway, and on to the final stretch back home.

# THE PRC

August quickly became September, and it was back to school. My dim social status stayed the same, but at least the schoolwork wasn't very challenging, so I had lots of free time to daydream and run. I joined the cross-country team again and reliably finished each race in the middle of the pack. By mid-October, the aches and pains and tendinitis I experienced after the run around the Hudson had died down, and running wasn't as physically challenging anymore, but mentally, it was still difficult to start a multi-hour run.

A couple of weeks after I got home from my run around the Hudson River, I worked up enough nerve to call Jose. It turned out he was serious about wanting to run with me and started going out for daily jogs the very afternoon I left the park. His big brother, who was actually younger but a lot taller, was looking to get in shape for basketball season and would go out with him most days. They lived close to Bronx Park, so they ran around there. He'd also convinced some of his cousins to occasionally go out with him; not the loco one, though.

We made a plan to do my run around the Hudson together the last weekend of October. The anticipation was killing me. Jose was my only real friend, and I couldn't wait; would I see Maria again? This time, I would be more prepared. I'd bring money, snacks, and toilet paper. With Jose and his big younger brother with me, I likely wouldn't get beat up on my way through Yonkers. Until then, I just kept running with the cross-country team and on my own. My goal was to not have to sleep in any parks.

The day of the run finally arrived. I woke up very early to catch a bus into the city. We planned to meet at The Cloisters Park at 7:00 AM and finish ten to twelve hours after that. It was a very cool and drizzly morning, but the weather report was for the rain to pass by midday. It was a perfect day for a long run. I arrived at the park ten minutes early, but Jose, his brother Andrew, and his two cousins Matty and Luis were already there. There were also two other boys who I didn't know were coming. The first was Leo, who was short and skinny like Jose and me, and carried around a very serious facial expression. The second was Carlos, who was taller and a little overweight and seemed too happy for someone about to start a forty-mile run on a rainy day. His general condition and happy demeanor convinced me that he had never run before.

After the introductions, I took Jose aside for a minute and asked him if his two friends knew what they were getting themselves into. Jose assured me they did and said Carlos was always great at any sport he tried out for. In reality, none of them knew what they were getting into. I managed to also blissfully forget how painful my first run around the Hudson was, but I was starting to remember again as the time to do it again neared. I didn't want to discourage anybody, so I just tried to keep in good spirits and helped Jose gather everybody together.

Public speaking always made me extremely nervous, but I felt I needed to say something, so I started with the facts. "The route is to run to the George Washington bridge over to New Jersey, and ..."

Matty interrupted, "Jose mapped it all out for us already, but what is our name?" I looked a little confused, so he continued. "You know, the name of our gang?"

I mumbled, "I didn't know we are a gang."

Leo joined in with, "You started this, so you get to name us."

They were all looking at me expectantly, except for big Andrew, who had a smirk on his face. I recovered quickly and said, "We are the Palisades Running Club, or PRC."

Leo smiled, "Cool. We're the PRC. It sounds like a rap group."

Matty pursed his lips into a soft frown and nodded coolly, seeming to approve of the rapper vibe. He had a nice medium sized afro going so could plausibly rap on the side. The rest of the PRC all looked satisfied too, so off we went.

Running South towards the George Washington Bridge, everybody was in high spirits, excited to be on this adventure. Andrew had an inconvenienced look on his face, but I think he was enjoying himself too. Out of all of us, he was the only non-volunteer. Their parents insisted that Andrew go with Jose. I was doing alright also, even though I had a pretty heavy pack on. Everybody had brought snacks, but I was the only one with a pack, so I ended up carrying everything. The weight of the pack dragged me down a little, but it was a small sacrifice to be in my own gang.

It was still only drizzling, but the wind picked up when we were crossing the bridge, and we all got soaked. We needed to run a little faster to stay warm and get off the bridge, but Carlos was starting to have problems. He was still trying to project a jovial demeanor, but I could see the strain on his face. He also slowed down considerably after the first mile and was breathing very heavily. When we finally finished the crossing, he immediately knelt down, right there on the sidewalk, and started puking. He must have really fueled up for the run since a lot came out of him.

It wasn't that we weren't sympathetic, but the puke was chunky and smelled horrible. If we hadn't backed away, we would have all been puking in a few seconds. The wind was blowing to the north, so we all went South. Matty was the first to say something, "That's fucking gross, Carlos. What the fuck did you eat for breakfast?"

Carlos croaked, "Just some bacon, eggs, pancakes, milk, ..."

I'm pretty sure there was more, but he didn't have the energy to list it all. He clearly couldn't go on.

Leo interjected, "Come on, Carlos, get up so we can get off this bridge. I'm freezing."

Carlos looked up at Leo, with a quick pout, but he managed to stagger up onto unsteady legs. We really should have gone over to help him, but some of the puke had dribbled down his shirt and somehow, he'd gotten his hands in it. We all made our way off the bridge where Carlos found a cleanish-looking puddle to wash up the best he could. Somewhat restored, he stated the obvious, "I don't think I can keep going."

Luis finally spoke up, dejected, "Are we heading back already? My sister said we would all fail. I guess she was right."

"We don't all have to quit. Can someone just walk back with Carlos so the rest of us can keep going?" Jose asked, a little angrily. Andrew actually nodded in agreement and asked who would go back with him.

Nobody volunteered. Carlos was still looking very pale and shaky and didn't look like he could walk all the way back across the bridge, anyway. I knew there was a bus station along the highway close by that could take him across the bridge, and from there he could catch a subway back home, so I suggested we do that. Fortunately, Carlos perked up a little at the idea. He didn't want to ruin our plans, and this was a solution. He didn't have any money, so I gave him five dollars for the fare.

By the time we got Carlos on his way back home, a full hour had passed since he got sick and two hours since we'd started. It was already 9:30 AM, and we had barely made any headway along the course. But now, we were going again, and without Carlos, we could keep a faster pace. The next leg of our route was around seven miles and went from Fort Lee to the marina along the Hudson where I had the run-in with Joe and his officer. We made good time, for us amateurs at least, and arrived at the marina a little before 11 AM.

The rain stopped and the sun came out, so we decided to take a short break. We had all recovered from the puking incident and had our appetites back. I dumped all the food out of my pack onto a picnic table and grabbed the bag of gorp I'd brought. Luis and Leo both had bags of chips and sandwiches but decided to save the sandwiches for later, and just munched down their chips like starving animals. Jose and Andrew had by far the best food, with homemade tortillas and tamales, courtesy of their mom and Maria. They made the same calculation and saved the tamales. It left me thinking I could have done better than just a big bag of gorp.

Luis stared at my bag and said, "Can I try some of that?" It turns out my bag of peanuts, raisins, and M&M's was popular, as after Luis grabbed a handful, everybody else dug in and grabbed some too. It was a big bag, but they left me with only a little for the rest of the day. I didn't know these guys that well yet, so I just took the last handful for myself and tossed the now-empty bag in the garbage without complaining.

As we were getting back up and ready to leave, Joe and his blue coveralls came by and unnecessarily hassled us about cleaning up after ourselves. This provoked Andrew to say, "What do you think we're doing, pops?"

Matty joined in, "Yo, go hassle someone else."

Joe mumbled that he was going to call the police and walked away. Matty said, "Jose told me you got hassled here before, was that the guy?"

I ignored the question and, in a panic, said, "We got to get out of here now! He wasn't bluffing about calling the cops."

Andrew and Matty looked at me sideways, like they weren't so sure we had anything to worry about, but everybody else was wide-eyed and moved quickly to get ready. I stuffed all the food back in my pack and led the gang to the trail up the cliffs. I wanted to get us as far away as possible before the cops arrived. Unfortunately, when we got up the trail and to the parking lot at the park entrance, there was a police car and two officers waiting for us. Our first instinct was to run back into the woods, but we all knew hiding in the woods until they went away wasn't a good option.

I was never good at being respectful to authority and felt a little sick to the stomach with nervousness, but I started to step forward to speak for the group anyway. Fortunately, Jose beat me to it, with Luis by his side, and respectfully started with, "Hello officers, how can we help you?"

The taller cop surveyed our group and answered, "I have a report that you six boys were down at the marina causing trouble and creating a disturbance."

Jose humbly reputed, "Sir, I think there may have been a misunderstanding. We are all part of a running club and stopped at the marina for a quick rest and a bite to eat. We didn't mean to bother anyone, and we cleaned up after ourselves when we left. We just want to continue our run back home."

It seemed like Jose had some practice talking to police officers, I knew I couldn't have been so calm. I looked over toward Andrew and Matty. They stood there with pursed lips, looking pissed, so I hoped they could keep it together and let Jose continue to smooth things out.

The officer seemed to relax a bit and asked, "Where are you all from?"

We each replied one at a time, with me telling them I was from Demarest, and the others all stating they were from the Bronx.

Anticipating his next question about why we were all there, I clumsily interjected, "We are doing a run around the Hudson, we started in New York and will finish there later. We are just quickly passing through."

"Alright, you, from Demarest, what is your name?" asked the police officer. After giving him my name, which he wrote down, he continued, "If I get any more calls about you or your friends causing trouble, I'll take you in and keep you at the station until all your parents come and pick you up. Is that clear?"

Jose and Luis enthusiastically said, "Yes, Sir!" simultaneously. The rest of us just looked down at the ground and mumbled our acknowledgments.

We all stood there awkwardly for another few seconds before the officer nodded his head to the left and told us we could go. He didn't have to tell us twice. We all high-tailed it out of there with an extra burst of adrenaline and silently made our way north up Route 9W. In fact, we didn't say much for the next hour until we got to the turn-off of 9W.

After the turn-off Matty exhaustedly said, "Man, I've got to stop soon. My feet and back are killing me." Everybody else, except Jose, agreed that we couldn't go much further without a break. I realized I was hurting too now, that I'd had a minute to self-assess.

"Just a little ways down the road, there is a good place to stop and rest and eat lunch," I told the group. Matty complained a bit, but I assured him that the stop was just around the corner. Unfortunately, it was a little more than that, so Matty started to really hassle me about my sense of distance. Luis even joined in a little, while Jose, Leo, and Andrew just gutted it out.

Fortunately, after around a mile, we got to the town center and parked ourselves in a park by the water. All of us plopped down on our backs and didn't move for several minutes. All of us, except for Andrew that is, who just sat calmly upright. He didn't like to project weakness, but I could tell from how he was limping along at the end that he was hurting just as much as the rest of us.

Matty didn't move his body, but he had plenty of energy to move his mouth and complain. There were lots of grunts, groans, and curse words, mostly directed at Jose and me. To sum up, he couldn't believe we'd made him do this. Jose rejected the idea he had made Matty come on the run, and they argued. Finally, Leo had had enough and dejectedly stated, "Just shut up." He bore a long frown, looking like he might cry.

Andrew angrily got involved with a quick, "You are both assholes."

I wasn't sure who the two assholes were in his opinion, but I needed to get things back under control, so I got up and announced, "Let's eat!" I dumped the lunch contents right on the ground and after a quick, "What the fuck did you pour our food onto the ground for?" from Matty. They all stopped bellyaching and grabbed their food.

They guzzled down almost everything they had like they hadn't eaten in years. No wonder everybody was so grumpy. Their mood quickly got better after getting some sustenance. My mood got more depressed, however, since I had nothing to eat. They'd eaten all my gorp back at the marina. Jose finally noticed this and asked me where my lunch was. I reminded them of what had happened back at the marina.

Leo, who was now fully recovered from his partial breakdown, blamed me by saying, "You should have brought more than just a bag of peanuts." He wasn't wrong, but despite my strong desire to reply with a rude remark, I did not want to provoke him. I wasn't good with confrontation. We still had a long way to go before we got home. It was now almost one o'clock, and we were probably only halfway through the route.

Jose was down to the last half of one of his tamales and kindly offered it to me, which I enthusiastically accepted. It wasn't nearly enough, though, but I spotted an ice cream shop across the street and let them know where I was going. That perked everybody up even more and we headed over.

I got a bag of chips and two scoops of chocolate ice cream in a cone. Everybody else also got ice cream plus other sweets. When it came to paying, it turned out only Jose and I had enough money to pay for everything. Luis, Leo, and Matty assured us that they would pay us back, but I had my doubts.

After overfilling ourselves with lunch, ice cream, other junk food, and wisecracks, we had another problem. We all needed to nap. It was early afternoon, and we had a very long way to go still, so we resigned ourselves to the task at hand; stiffly, and with a few limps, we got back to our run. The next two and a half miles to the entrance to the Tappan Zee Bridge was brutal. In addition to having to loosen up our muscles again, we all started cramping up. Filling our bellies with ice cream seemed like a good idea at the time, but now we were paying for it. We stopped several times on the way to the bridge as one by one we went down with severe stomach cramps. Luckily, before starting our crossing, we found a public bathroom, and a few of us, including me, made good use of it.

As we started our almost four-mile bridge crossing, we had mostly recovered from our cramps, but we were all weak and tired. As usual, Matty was the most vocal about it and was driving the rest of us nuts. He finally curbed his complaining somewhat after Andrew and Luis threatened to throw him off the "fucking bridge." Despite our sorry condition, the air was still and cool, and the sun was out. It could have been much worse. After forty-five minutes of consistent running, we made it off the bridge and close to the place where I'd spent the night on my first run.

It was 3:00 PM, and we all had renewed energy from knowing we were back in New York, so we kept going at a slow pace. We still had fourteen miles to go. The pace was very slow, since we'd decided that we were going to stay in a single group. Luis and Andrew seemed to hit a wall after another few miles and we had to keep stopping to rest so they could catch their breath and nurse their wounds. I was happy not to be the weak link, but in truth, I wasn't much better off. Like everybody else, I had pains shooting up from my feet. I had blisters on blisters and did not know if I could actually make it to the end.

The eight-plus miles to Yonkers took us another three hours. It was now 6:00 PM and the sun was going down.

I was so tired, I felt like I was in a bubble. I'm pretty sure Matty started complaining again, but I barely noticed. I was also too tired to care that I was back in the place I got beat up the first time around. At this point, I was worried about open rebellion among the group, but fortunately, everyone was too tired and in too much pain to even complain anymore. We looked like a group of zombies. Jose tried to cheer everybody up by mentioning that we had fewer than five miles to go before we were done, but that only got him death threats.

After another four hours of running, walking, and limping along, we finally made it back to The Cloisters. It should have been a celebration, but it was after 10:00 PM and we were all cold and miserable. After some time sitting on the park benches, we slowly started to get our spirits back. Not happy spirits, but Matty managed to tell Jose that this run could have been the stupidest thing he ever came up with. Andrew managed a quick "shut up" to Matty, and Leo was already determining how we would all get home.

"The bus is still running if we get going now," Leo suggested.

Everybody made their way back to their feet, except me. Jose noticed and said, "You can stay at my place tonight."

"Really?" I asked, elated. For all the planning we had done ahead of time to start our journey, we hadn't considered what we would all do after we'd finished. We just assumed we would all grab a bite and head back to our homes, not realizing that we wouldn't finish until late at night and be so crippled. "Okay," I said gratefully.

We limped a half mile to a bus stop that would take us out of Manhattan and across to the Bronx. Once there, it was just a short walk to the neighborhood where they all lived. Since it was Saturday night, it was rowdy on the streets. We walked by lots of open shops and bars. The sidewalks were crowded with boisterous people, many of them drinking. A couple of times, a reveler would shout out a greeting to our gang members. One of them even came up to Matty, he looked over at me and said, "Who's the white kid?"

Matty simply replied, "He's with us." After looking me over like I smelled bad, which I probably did, he let us pass.

In no time, we arrived at Jose and Andrew's building, which also happened to be Luis's building, and exited the chaos of the street. As soon as we stepped into the foyer beyond the entrance and the doors were closed behind us, I felt a sudden sense of relief. I didn't realize how on edge walking through the anarchy of the Bronx on a Saturday night had made me.

Immediately after entering Jose and Andrew's apartment, we were besieged by their mom. After chewing them out in Spanish, she noticed me standing behind Andrew. Jose quickly said, "Ma, this is my friend Simon I've talked to you about. It was too late for him to get back to Jersey, so we invited him to crash here."

After realizing that she had company, Jose's Mother immediately composed herself and offered me her hand, and said, "It's so nice to finally meet you, Simon. You are welcome to stay here."

"Thank you, Mrs. ...?" shoot, I didn't even know Jose's last name.

"Just call me Mrs. Perez," she graciously interjected.

She promptly went off to the kitchen to make us some food. Jose smiled at me and said, "You saved our butts, man. She would have really been on us if you weren't here." Apparently, they'd never mentioned to Ma that they might not get home until late at night. I wondered if the feast she was pulling out of the fridge and heating up was for my benefit, but it was just as likely she didn't like her kids going to bed hungry.

The feast turned out to be leftover rice and beans with a side of chicken thighs. Everything was very flavorful and plentiful. We dug in like animals, which prompted Mrs. Perez to say, "Slow down, you are going to make yourselves sick." There was no slowing down, however. We were three teenage boys who had just finished a forty-mile run. After eating, we made our way to Jose and Andrews' room, where they shared a bunk bed. I got a nice quilt and some pillows and sheets on the floor. After a few minutes of farting and joking around, we quickly fell asleep, completely exhausted.

I was awoken the next morning by Mrs. Perez clapping her hands and saying very loudly, "Vamos, Vamos, ...." After she'd verified that both Jose and Andrew were grunting "Ah's and Eh's," she left us alone, but didn't close the door. We were all stiff and probably looked like hell. I confirmed that a little later when I saw my puffy, red face and droopy eyes in the bathroom mirror. It was Sunday, and church services were at 10:00 AM, so unfortunately, sleeping in and resting was not an option. I had a few more minutes to laggardly lie in my quilt before Jose and Andrew finished cleaning up and were allowed to eat breakfast.

When we made our way to the table, Maria and Mr. Perez were already just finishing. Maria gave me a smile and said, "Hi, Simon," which I insanely interpreted as "Maybe she loves me?" Mr. Perez said, "Simon, it's so nice to meet you. Jose has told me a lot about you. Tell me about your run yesterday?"

I started, "It was really hard, but everyone made it to the end and had fun."

Both Jose and Andrew simultaneously snorted right after I said fun. Mr. Perez looked them over and said, "It wasn't fun?"

"It might have been the most painful thing I've ever done in my life. My feet are covered in blisters," Jose stated.

"Well, I'm proud of you boys. Most kids around here don't do anything but cause trouble," Mr. Perez said.

I didn't know much about the other kids who lived in the neighborhood, but Jose seemed to agree, and his Ma nodded in agreement. Andrew only seemed to be paying attention to his food. Maria had gotten up and fixed the three of us large plates of eggs, bacon, and flour tortillas. We all also got large glasses of milk. Despite the large meal right before bed, I was still hungry for as much food as I could get. My table manners fell by the wayside as I shoveled the food into my mouth, but Andrew was actually picking up eggs with his hands to get them into his mouth faster, so I don't think they noticed me. At least I used a fork.

Mrs. Perez noticed too and chided Andrew, "Andrew, get your hands out of your food right now."

Andrew complied but didn't miss a mouthful while deftly switching from hands to fork. Right after breakfast, it was time to go. The five members of the Perez family were all dressed up nicely in their Sunday best, but I still had my smelly clothes on from the run the day before. This probably saved me from being asked to join them.

Outside, the chaos from the previous night was replaced by sedate streets. There were a few bums here and there sleeping off a night of inebriating substances, and the typical mildewy smell of the city. Unlike the night before, I didn't feel like I was going to be jumped at any minute. When I got to the station entrance, we said our goodbyes and I walked down into the subway. Luckily, it was quiet down there too, so my ride home on the train and then the bus was uneventful. By now, I had forgotten most of the pain and suffering we had experienced on our run and was just left reflecting on all the fun we'd had. I was already looking forward to doing it again.

# BACK TO THE GRIND

After all the planning and anticipation that went into my run with Jose and his friends, coming back home and going to school was a little bit of a letdown. Cross-country season was ending, and I wasn't looking forward to wrestling. My solution was to just quit wrestling and continue to run on my own. My second time around the Hudson went much better than the first (one day vs. three days), but it was still more painful than I wanted it to be.

I ran every day after school and did longer runs on the weekends. Running after school was a little tricky because I had a heavy backpack full of books to carry home. I didn't want to leave my books at school, then come back for them after the run, and then take the sports bus or walk home. My solution to the bouncing backpack problem was to wrap a bungee cord around my torso to hold the backpack firmly against me. Then I just did my run in my sneakers and jeans I wore to school.

Running with a heavy back was painful at first; I had to build back up to running long distances over a few weeks while my back adapted to the pressure of the pack. Once I got used to it, my pack-heavy four to five-mile after-school runs made my pack-less weekend runs in actual sweats seem like I was running on air. I regularly did ten-mile runs on both Saturdays and Sundays.

My parents just assumed I came home late on weekdays and was out on weekends because I was still going to wrestling practices and meets. They never asked about how practice or how a competition went, so I didn't even have to regularly lie; just occasionally. Maybe telling Stepbad about my running exploits would impress him, but to my way of thinking, it was none of my parents' business. It was my thing. Anyway, he would likely get hung up on me quitting wrestling instead of regarding my long-distance running as an achievement. I know my audience.

I talked to Jose on the phone multiple times a week. I usually worked at least one day or evening over the weekend, so sometimes on the other day I would go over to his apartment, and we would run together. Out of the original PRC gang, only Jose and Matty continued running. The other members had enough after that one experience, but once a PRC member, always a PRC member. We decided admission to our very exclusive club required a member to finish the run around the Hudson as one segment, though you could take multiple days to finish it, like I did on my first try. You just could not leave the route at any time until the loop was completed. This meant that the PRC stayed at six members, but we had plans for expansion.

The best part of going to the Bronx to run with Jose and Matty was hanging out at Jose's apartment afterward. Sometimes, if I went there on a Saturday, I would also stay for dinner and the night. Jose's parents didn't feel comfortable sending me back home alone on the subway if it got later than early evening. We did get to leave the apartment and experience the excitement of the street, as long as there was a bunch of us together. When we were out on the street, it was always at least Jose, Matty, and me, and usually Luis, Leo, and Carlos too. Andrew had his own friends he wanted to hang out with.

On one of our Sunday runs, we decided to run to Yonkers and back. The total route there and back would be thirteen miles. We managed to complete the first leg to Yonkers in just over an hour, and as was our custom, we would stop for junk food halfway through the run. Today it was donuts. It was late March and one of the nicest days for running that year so far. It was around 50 degrees, clear, and sunny.

As I sat there in the park eating my jelly donut, I noticed some winos at the other end of the park doing wino things, like drinking and stumbling around. One of the winos I knew all too well. It was Red. He looked more weathered than I remembered him and less menacing. He was actually pretty pathetic. Matty noticed me staring at them across the park and said, "What you looking at over there?"

I replied, "You see that bum with the red hair and big nose?" Matty and Jose nodded. "That is the asshole that beat me up when I first did the Hudson run last August."

Matty laughed, "You got beat up by that pathetic wino!?!"

"Well, he was much bigger back then," I shot back, embarrassed.

I don't think Matty was convinced, and I hoped he didn't lose all respect for me; instead, he suggested we teach him a lesson.

This was a chance for me to get my dignity back, so I smartly replied, "Yo, let's fuck him up." It was easy being brave when you had the numbers on your side.

After a brief moment, Matty let us know the plan. "First, we need to get him away from the other bums and someplace private. Junkies love sweets, so we use our last donut to lure him to those trees over there." Jose and I just nodded enthusiastically. We were in the presence of an obvious criminal mastermind. He continued, "Simon, you know him, so you lure him with the donut, and me and Jose will wait behind the trees. When he gets close, we'll knock him to the ground and beat on him until he cries."

Knowing I was going to be the point man immediately made me nervous, but I couldn't look like a wimp, so I just nodded my head in agreement with eyes that were maybe opened a little too wide.

"Is that going to be a problem?" Matty asked accusingly.

"No!" I firmly replied.

Jose interjected, "What if we get in trouble?"

Matty, with a small sideways nod, just looked at him like he was stupid and waved Jose to follow him, leaving me with the last donut. After I saw them get situated behind a tree not far from the wino pack, I took a few deep breaths and, with no plan, started walking over to the pack. Luckily, Red was already at the edge of the group and the other bums seemed occupied in their own minds.

The Zombies were currently docile. I got within ten feet of Red and said, "Hey, Red," in a loud whisper. He didn't turn to look at me. Maybe he didn't go by Red? I tried again, "Hey Douchebag, where's Shane?" I don't know if it was identifying him as Douchebag that did the trick or using his friend's name, but he looked over at me.

I continued, "Douchebag, want a donut?" I waved the donut in front of me and even blew off some of the sugar topping to heighten the effect. I had him hooked. Now it was time to reel him in.

"Come on, Douchebag, the donut is yours if you can get me." While slowly walking backwards towards the trees, I repeated "Douchebag, Douchebag, Douchebag, ..."

"You fucker!" He seemed to suddenly come to life and stumbled toward me fast, or fast for a strung-out douchebag. This was going swimmingly – and then I tripped over a root and landed flat on my ass. Red was on me faster than I would have thought possible. He wasn't physically hurting me, but I was gasping for fresh air; the stench was unbearable. I felt his greasiness rubbing off onto my skin, and I think he'd crapped and peed himself sometime in the last few days.

It seemed like we were attached for days, but I think it was only a few seconds before I managed to flip him over and stand up. That is when Matty and Jose sprang out from behind the tree. Red was on his back, looking like a stuck turtle, when Matty first kicked him in the ribs. Jose looked at Matty a little shocked, but he soon recovered and then kicked him too, though only halfheartedly. I also joined in with a much fuller heart. Something in me snapped and I just kept kicking him in the torso while Matty and Jose moved to his legs. Then Matty unzipped his pants and started peeing on him. A little got on my foot, which pulled me out of my violent trance. I joined in and started peeing on him too. Jose didn't.

That was fortunate since it meant Jose was paying attention to what was happening around us. Around a hundred yards away, a cop was running straight towards us. The winos had noticed us too and seemed pretty agitated, though they didn't come to help their buddy. The three of us did what we did best and took off running. Every bit of energy and strength we'd built up over the previous months of training now came to fruition. Occasionally, I looked back, but never spotted the cop. We ended up in a dense wooded area and stopped to take measure.

All three of us were pumped with adrenaline and felt better than ever. Matty was laughing and even Jose had a big stupid smile painted across his face. This was the most fun I'd had in my whole life. It turned out part of why Matty was laughing was at my expense. "You tripping and that bum landing on top of you was the funniest thing I ever seen, dude! I bet you have AIDS!"

"Fuck you!" I replied without anger. I did start to feel a little uneasy though, what if Red gave me some sort of disease?

"We need to get out of Yonkers before they call in reinforcements," Jose stated urgently.

"What you talking about," Matty replied.

"The cop we outrun will be back with squad cars and reinforcements."

Jose's analysis made sense to me, but Matty confidently said, "They don't give a shit about some bum, but whatever. Let's go."

We turned South and started our run back. After we were safely a couple of miles out of Yonkers, we slowed down to our normal pace and spent the rest of the run back to the Bronx reliving our day's adventure. By the time we shared the story with our other friends, Red was much bigger and more menacing. He had muscles on muscles and super energy fueled by coke. We fought him off like superheroes and probably saved some poor women and children from Red as a bonus. Escaping capture while being chased by what must have been a dozen cops was also quite a feat.

# THE HUDSON RIVER ULTRA

My meetup with Jose and Matty was not just about running. We'd also decided to organize an ultra-marathon using my route around the Hudson River, and we wanted to get it done before senior year was over and we all went in separate directions. We would host the race on May 25th, which was Memorial Day weekend, the race would start at 8:00 AM sharp, and you had to be a PRC member to run. We decided to add a second way to join the PRC. You could finish the run around the Hudson, or you could pay us $5.00 on race day and get your bib with a number.

Out of the original PRC members, only Jose, Matty, and I were running in the marathon. We were able to recruit the other members and family to help out in other ways. Maria, Mrs. Perez, and Matty's Dad would collect the fees and hand out the bibs. I found a store that sold numbered bibs cheaply along with containers of pins. Luis worked in his school's administration office and had access to an old ditto machine, which he could use to print copies of the flyer promoting the race.

I drew out a simple map of the route. I added some flourishes, like cliffs to represent the Palisades, and major attractions, like the Palisades Park Marina, some of the other parks and city centers along the way, and of course, the two bridges and the Hudson itself. Included in the map were all the details, including mile markers, the start and finish (The Cloisters Park), and the price of admission. The name of the race was "The Hudson River Ultra-40." Luis printed out 500 copies of my flyer, and we spread them around our schools and as many other places as we could think of. We made sure to research where other runners in clubs ran and hung out so we could get our flyers into those places as well.

Meanwhile, Jose, Matty, and I kept on training for the race and hoped that runners would actually show up on race day. Some of the kids at our schools asked questions about the race after seeing the flyer, but beyond that, we had no way of knowing if there was other interest. I did get a semi-firm commitment from two members of my cross-country team, so possibly two people would show up on race day.

May 25th finally arrived. To get an early start, I left for Jose's apartment first thing after school on Friday and stayed over at his family's apartment Friday night. We were all really excited about the race but also worried that there would be a poor showing and we would get embarrassed. Mrs. Perez assured us that we had nothing to worry about and had been praying all week for a successful race. Even Andrew expressed some regret for not joining us for the run, but when I reminded him that he didn't have to regret not joining us and could just come and run with us, he quickly backtracked and said he couldn't because it would interfere with his baseball.

On Saturday morning, we all fueled up and headed to the park, not knowing what to expect. At 7:00 AM, it was only us and our helpers, and we started to get a little worried. At 7:15 AM, Luis and his dad showed up, but neither were running. At that point, Matty started to freak out a bit and started going on about how nobody was showing up, and he would never live this down. Since Jose and I were also freaking out, his attitude didn't help things.

Then, at 7:32 AM, we saw a large group of adults in shorts and t-shirts walking up the path toward us. "Look at that, they look like runners to me, man!" I exclaimed excitedly. When they got closer, I saw that some of their t-shirts had "The Bronx Runners Club" printed on them. There were sixteen of them, ten men and six women. A few of them were fairly old and hunched over, so you could tell they had lots of miles on them. Jose got up first and ran over to them to ask if they were here for the run.

"Yes, why else would we be here?" two of the men said in unison. One of the women slapped the guy on the shoulder and said to play nice.

"Sorry, just go over to that table over there to register and get your numbered bib. We start at eight," Jose informed them.

As they walked over, we noticed individuals and groups of people starting to filter in from all sides, and by 7:45 AM, there was a line forming at registration that was twenty people deep. The crowds also drew some unwanted attention. Two police officers walked over to the registration table and started asking what was going on. Mrs. Perez let them know we were hosting a race, and one of the officers asked if we had permits to do that. This led to an argument between the cops, Mrs. Perez, and Mr.

Sanchez (Matty's Dad). The cops weren't having any of it and we started to worry they would shut us down. Other runners also started to notice, and a few interjected themselves, which meant things were starting to get ugly.

That's when Luis's Dad came to the rescue. He was a Lieutenant at the 44th precinct and quickly separated the crowd from the two officers, taking the officers to the side. I'm not sure what he told them, but they backed off. Later, I found out that Luis's Dad had promised to take them both out to lunch at a steak house if they let our non-permitted event slide. A steak dinner for two was probably less hassle and money than actually trying to get a permit from the city, so a little corruption was a great solution to the problem.

Eight o'clock came and went, but people were still filing in, so we delayed the start. By twenty after, nobody was left in the line, and we had 103 runners, including Jose, Matty, and me. I got on the megaphone and asked everyone to gather at an open section of the park to start the race at 8:30 AM. We didn't have a formal starting line, so we all just packed together in the same space to start the race. I then handed the megaphone to Luis who yelled at the top of his lungs for everyone to get ready. Then he counted down from ten and yelled, "Go!" Jose, Matty, and I started at the front of the pack, but were quickly eclipsed by some of the faster runners. By the time we got to the George Washington Bridge, we were still ahead of around three-quarters of the runners, so we felt pretty good about things. I hoped the runners in front knew the way. Our goal was to finish the race in under seven hours.

Running along the palisades, we were with the main group of runners. It reminded me of a bicycle race where I was in the peloton, making the most of the slipstream. The runners that passed us were no longer in sight, and I knew some runners had already dropped off the back of the peloton. By the time we got to the Palisades Marina, we were nine miles into the race, and it barely seemed like any time had passed at all. We were running at a seven-mile an hour pace, so arrived there in just over an hour and a quarter. If it were just the three of us, we would have stopped for a rest and some snacks, but we felt pressure to just keep going with all the other runners around us.

None of us had ever sustained a pace like this for so long, so by the time we ran another eight miles to Piermont, another hour and 15 minutes had passed, and I had to stop. Lots of runners in the peloton were pretty talkative, but Jose, Matty, and me mostly just concentrated on keeping the pace. When we reached Piermont, I pointed towards the park where we'd stopped the last time we ran this loop; Matty just said he was glad I was the first one to break. Both of them were also ready to stop.

Since we were keeping pace, the whole group just followed us like sheep into the main park, and when we stopped, there was some confusion and other runners asked us what was going on. I called out that I was just stopping to eat some food, many of the other runners decided this was a good idea and also stopped to eat and use the public restroom. A group of around ten runners just kept going. After around ten minutes, a guy with a raggedy beard and a white sleeveless shirt, which was now well stained, came up to us and introduced himself as John. "I've been in a lot of these types of races and if we don't get going soon, people are going to start stiffening up and will not be able to finish the race," John informed us.

"Okay, but I usually loosen back up after a few minutes," I replied.

"You're young," was John's only reply.

Jose understood what he was saying, so he got up and let everyone, now spread around the park, know that we were going to get going in a couple of minutes. John gave us a little thank-you salute, and we got going again, but at a slower pace to start. Just as we were leaving, a few of the stragglers caught up with us, so the peloton got back some of the people we had lost when we stopped. By the time we reached the Tappan Zee Bridge, we were back up to our seven-minute a mile pace. At this juncture in the race, the three of us were now in the middle of a very stretched-out peloton, running along the side of the bridge. Looking at the long line of runners ahead and behind us, we could really see how amazing the race we conceived of had turned out. I pointed this out to Matty and Jose and it gave us the extra energy we needed to make the final push back to The Cloisters.

Two hours and forty minutes after the lunch break, we had run another sixteen miles and reached downtown Yonkers. With about fifty of us in tow, we bottle-necked around the intersections getting through the city but still managed to run the final six miles to the finish line in just over an hour. With the peloton, we finished the race in seven hours. Maria let us know that thirty-three runners had finished before we arrived, and after counting the runners that finished in our group, we confirmed that a total of seventy-eight runners had finished the race so far.

When we got to the finish line, we were in for some surprises. The first one was that Mrs. Perez had bought one hundred engraved medals. The center of the medal contained a little montage of the George Washington Bridge with the Palisades in the background. Along the top was written "The Hudson River Ultra-40," and along the bottom was written "The Palisades Running Club." She also bought two blue, red, and white ribbons for the first, second, and third place men's and women's finishers, respectively. Those she had already given out before we showed up. The first-place man finished in four hours and twenty-three minutes, while the second and third-place men were only three minutes behind. Since they finished at the same time, they flipped a coin to see which of the remaining two ribbons they would get. The first-place woman finished in four hours and fifty-three minutes, while the next two women finished around five and ten minutes after that. Everyone that finished got a medal, except for the last three, if they managed to finish, that was.

Word of our race had gotten out to various church groups and organizations in Bronx's Puerto Rican community, so by the time we got back to the park, a party was going on that reminded me of the first time I ran through the Cloisters Park and met Jose. There were lots of tables set up and people cooking food. My mouth watered from the smell of barbequed beef blowing in from multiple locations. People were sitting on lawn chairs, eating and drinking beer. There was even a face-painting station for the kids. Many of the runners were already taking full advantage of this and filling their plates and guzzling down beers.

Jose, Matty, and I were starving, so we got right in there and spent the next thirty minutes eating our way through all of the tables. We were constantly interrupted by runners coming up to congratulate us on a great race. I think they were especially impressed by the amazing spread of free food and booze they got just for finishing. Many of them told us they couldn't wait until we did it again next year, but I knew there was not going to be a next year; nevertheless, I kept that to myself to not spoil the festive mood. Matty did let one participant know that this was a one-time thing, but Jose and I quickly asked him to keep that to himself. He told us we were idiots, but went along with it anyway.

Slowly, as the afternoon turned to evening, almost everyone there, except for Jose, Matty, and Luis, had filtered out, and by 7:00 PM, it was just us. During the party, seventeen more runners had finished the race. At 8:15 PM, one more runner named Bob meandered in, so we clapped wholeheartedly for Bob and gave him his medal. At 8:30 PM, we decided to officially end the race, so a total of ninety-six runners finished the race and got their medals.

The next morning started like most other Sunday mornings when I stayed over at Jose's apartment. Mrs. Perez and Maria made us all a nice breakfast, then the

Perez family left for church, and I left for home back in New Jersey. Before going home, I decided to head back to Cloisters Park one more time to see if any other runners had shown up. I'm not sure why I decided to do that, since my guess was that any runners that finished in the middle of the night would be long gone, but something told me to go.

It was a mellow scene when I got there. Some joggers were running through the park and other people were walking their dogs and sitting on the park benches reading the paper. Away from the noise of the city, it was pretty quiet and peaceful. I sat on the grass for a few minutes to enjoy the fresh air before getting up to make my way to the bus station at the George Washington Bridge. Before I left the park, I took one last look back and saw a man in shorts and a t-shirt with one of the numbered bibs pinned to his chest, asleep against a tree.

I walked over and got down next to him and said, "Hey, man," while gently shaking his arm. He woke up a little startled and asked where he was and who I was. I told him I was one of the race organizers and asked him when he got here.

"Yes, I remember you. I'm not sure what time I finished, but it was just getting light. I just stopped here to rest for a few minutes. What time is it?"

I replied that it was almost 10:00 AM and asked him his name.

"Al, Al Rosen."

"I'm Simon, was there anybody else with you when you finished?" I asked.

61

"No, I was running with two women, and after we got over the Tappan Zee Bridge it was already dark and pretty late at night. They didn't feel comfortable finishing the race in the dark, so they called a family member to come and pick them up. I waited with them but decided to keep going." He then tried to get up and started cursing. "Shit, shit, shit, shit, shit, my legs are cramped, I can't get up. I think I have blisters."

"Yep, you're in for a bad few days, but here's your medal for finishing." I handed him a medal and that perked him up a bit, but I still had to help him get up and walk with him for several yards until he steadied himself. He then went off in the opposite direction from where I was going to, still cursing under his breath. With the information from Al, that accounted for 99 of the 103 runners that registered. I never found out what happened to the last four. Losing only four percent of the runners that started was a very good showing in my estimation, so I felt the whole venture was a resounding success.

# HIGHER LEARNING

I was lying on the ground looking up at the spinning stars. It was a clear crisp autumn night on campus. I could hear the murmur of loud music and shouting in the distant background as the parties in the fraternity quad were in full swing. I wasn't lying on the ground and admiring the stars because of my love of the astros or because of my admiration for the beauty of the universe, but because I was so drunk that I had fallen on my back. And it was really my head that was spinning, not the stars. I don't remember much about that evening, but I must have drunk a lot. I never drank before coming to college, but in the six weeks since I'd been there, I'd played a lot of catch up in this regard.

Shortly after the ultra-marathon, I graduated from high school and spent a busy summer working at a local golf club and heading into the city, often, to visit Jose and the rest of the gang. Summer passed and now I was attending college, catching up on all of the partying and drinking I missed out on in high school.

After an indeterminate amount of time, I pushed myself up on my hands and knees and tried to stand up. It was slow going, and I teetered a little bit as the ground seemed to shift under me, but I managed to get to my feet and stumble forward in the general direction of my dorm. Being in this state didn't feel good, but I'd gotten drunk at every party I'd attended so far anyway. The problem is that drinking beer is something to do at a party. If I'd remained sober, I would just have stood along the side of the wall looking awkward, but after a few drinks, I loosened up and acted normally for a few minutes until I had a few more drinks and stopped functioning.

Somehow, I made it back to my dorm room. There were some other people in the hallway making comments and jokes at my expense, but I could barely hear them. As soon as I got into my room and closed the door, I felt my bowels loosen. I was cognizant enough to know I had two plans of action. The first was to crap my pants, then pass out in bed and worry about the consequences in the morning, and the second was to crap somewhere else, then pass out in bed and worry about the consequences in the morning. I chose the latter and crapped in our room's little steel garbage can, before following through with the rest of the plan.

Word got out about the garbage can incident and became a popular talking point in some circles. My reaction to the teasing was to just deny it happened. I learned early in life that a great strategy to avoid trouble was to just deny, deny, deny until your adversary got tired of countering. It didn't matter whether the evidence was unequivocal or not. As the closest eyewitness to the event in question, my recollection mattered most. In this case, denying the undeniable was effective. What could have ruined me for my entire time on campus, died down to only someone occasionally reminding me of what I had done. A quick "What the fuck are you talking about," look usually put a quick stop to the asshole.

College life wasn't only about getting drunk, though. I went to class too and maybe even learned a thing or two between naps. In high school, I was a straight-A student, but by the time I got to college, I was burnt out. I was miserable; most of my professors were worse teachers than I was a student. I did well in my lone liberal arts history class and programming lab but bordered on the edge of failing my three other math and science classes. I had been interested in math and science before coming here, but my professors beat the interest out of me.

# PASSING

I finished my freshman year of college and managed to barely pass all my courses. Afterwards, I decided to go back to the Bronx where I was most comfortable. Leo, Luis, and Matty shared a two-bedroom apartment in their Bronx neighborhood and needed a fourth roommate to cover the rent. Matty helped me get a job at Santini's Deli where he worked. The job involved all aspects of the business, including unloading the delivery truck, stocking shelves, working the cash register, and making deliveries. It paid enough to cover my share of the rent and to eat, which was all I needed. The best part of the job was they gave me a free daily hero and bag of chips as part of my compensation. I enjoyed working at the deli much more than doing schoolwork, so I knew very quickly that I wasn't going back to college in the fall.

Jose was off for the summer too. He had a full scholarship to Fordham University, so he never left the Bronx either. He got a job at the university, which didn't pay well but allowed him to stay in his dorm room rent-free. This was the best summer of my life. Most Sunday nights I had family dinner at Jose's parents' apartment and went out drinking with the guys on Friday and Saturday nights. I managed to control my alcohol intake much better than at college. Part of that was we were all still underage, so we didn't want to bring attention to ourselves and get carded. We went to the bars and played the part of seasoned drinkers.

Jose, Matty, and I had stopped running together after the Hudson River ultra, but Jose and I decided to start again and ran Sunday mornings after he got back from church. Our runs were much shorter than in the past, all located in the parks around Fordham. Mostly, it was just a chance for us to hang out and spend some time together. After the run, we would usually meet up with some of the other guys for brunch at Jose's campus. His scholarship included a food allowance at the university's cafeterias, but he didn't use nearly all of it. Living so close to home, Mrs. Perez made sure he had decent food to eat, which meant there was plenty of money left over for him to take his friends to the main all-you-can-eat cafeteria on campus on Sundays.

Knowing that I hated my college and wasn't going back to it, Jose tried to convince me to transfer to Fordham. I started looking into it and even applied to their engineering school to take computer courses. I didn't really want to go back to school and was comfortable with my life as it was, working at the deli, but Jose gave me the hard sell. He was convinced that come fall I would be wishing I were back in school working on a career. That may have been high school Simon, but current Simon looked forward to eating his hero at Santini's deli more than he looked forward to hitting the books.

The day my life took a much different direction started out like every workday. I got up around 9:00 AM, quickly showered, and gobbled down a bagel and cream cheese.

It was a hot muggy August day and, as usual, the city stunk. My weekday shift at the deli was 11:00 AM until it closed at 8:00 PM. The first order of business was making sandwiches to help with the lunch rush. In mid-July, Mr. Santini trusted me enough to prepare food. I still had to do all my other jobs, but I got to those after the lunch rush.

It was around 3:00 PM and Matty and I were unloading boxes from the latest delivery when Andrew came into the store. His eyes were bloodshot; he looked like he had been crying. Andrew never cried and always walked around with a confident smirk on his face, so we knew something was very wrong and our hearts immediately dropped. We stopped working and stared at him while waiting for the news. He looked down at the ground and just said, "He's dead."

Matty immediately replied, "Who's dead?"

"Jose."

We stood there speechless for what seemed like several minutes but was probably only a few seconds. Matty then asked, "What do you mean?"

"I mean, Jose is dead," Andrew said slowly, enunciating each word, while staring directly at Matty.

I jumped in and said, "Where is he?"

"I just left the hospital, he's there."

"Are you sure he's dead, how do you know? What happened, Andrew?" Matty demanded loudly.

"The Doctor said so! He was hit by a car. The Doctor said he died immediately," Andrew shot back.

"They don't know shit. We need to get to the hospital now!" Matty responded.

I agreed with needing to get to the hospital. We quickly told Mr. Santini what was going on and ran all the way to St. Barnabas Hospital. It was only a few blocks from the deli. When we got there, Andrew led us to the emergency department. Mr. and Mrs. Perez and Maria were still there. Some of their friends had also started gathering in the lobby, so there was a large crowd of people there, all comforting the Perez family. When Maria saw Matty and I walk in, she ran over and hugged us both around the neck, saying over and over that she couldn't believe what had happened. When she let go my shoulder was damp.

I just pushed away a little and asked her, "Is he really gone?"

She just nodded her head. Tears were running down her eyes and her nose was red and running. My reaction was to just sit in the closest chair and stare into space. I didn't know how to handle it. Matty's reaction was more anger, and he started punching a chair, attracting attention from hospital security. Mr. Perez and Luis's Dad quickly calmed him down and Matty apologized to them, repeating that this couldn't be true. Out of all of us teenagers, Jose was the nicest and most well-loved by everyone in his neighborhood. As the lobby filled up with people wanting to comfort his family, eventually the hospital staff had to ask everyone but the immediate family to move outside, where we all held vigil for several more hours before people started leaving.

The next morning, Matty didn't want to leave his room, but I needed to get out, so I started my walk to work like every morning. I left earlier than usual, so I was just randomly walking around, killing time, when I passed a recruitment office for the Army. Without much thought, I walked in and signed up. I had two days to prepare before I was to report to a bus stop in Brooklyn where I would be bussed to Fort Benning, Georgia to go through basic training.

After that impulsive choice, I went to work as normal and finished out the day before telling Mr. Santini what I had done. He understood, wished me luck, and told me to come back in the morning to collect my final paycheck.

Leo, Luis, and Matty weren't as understanding that night when I told them I'd signed up for the military. In fact, Matty felt betrayed, like he'd now lost a second friend in two days. I never considered that, but he was right in feeling that way. I should have stayed longer to mourn. It was only after speaking with Matty that I realized I wouldn't even make the funeral. I couldn't reverse my decision or delay my departure, so unfortunately, this was how my life in the Bronx would end. I didn't regret joining the Army. Without Jose around, I just needed to leave.

I did make sure to stop by the Perez household the next day after collecting my final paycheck. They weren't upset that I would miss the funeral and accepted my decision. The only things left to do after that were to close my bank account and turn my meager savings into cash for the journey, and then pack up as much as would fit in one day pack for my trip. I boxed the rest of my stuff and mailed it to my parents' home in New Jersey. The next day, at 7:00 AM, I was on a bus to Georgia.

# Basic Training

I stepped off the bus and was immediately engulfed by the heaviness of the hot humid air, and within seconds I felt sticky and was dripping with sweat. It was early in the day in August, and I'd never felt anything like this. New York City also got hot and humid in the summer, but this was on another level. The bus dropped me off in downtown Columbus, Georgia, where after a long wait, I caught a shuttle to the base with around twenty other recruits who had also arrived that day from various destinations.

As soon as I stepped off the second bus, I was surrounded by Drill Sergeant's yelling at me and everyone else to line up and stand up straight. This was our 'welcome' to Fort Benning, and we all just stood there holding our bags in the afternoon heat for several minutes. I was better off than most, since I just had a single small day pack to hold, while most of the recruits had brought larger duffels and suitcases overstuffed with things they probably wouldn't need. By the time they marched us to the admissions building, one recruit had fainted, and another had dropped to the ground crying. This drew the ire of the Drill Sergeants to the boy crying on the ground and the two adjacent recruits. The crying soldier was mocked for not being able to stay standing and acting like a baby, and the other recruits were disciplined for not assisting their fellow recruit.

Strangely, they ignored the guy who was out cold. I guess it wasn't fun to scream at someone who couldn't hear you.

After the welcome, we marched to a building for our initial processing. The recruit who fainted was dragged along by two other recruits, and the kid who dropped to the ground crying was left behind; I never saw him again. The building we were led into was air-conditioned, which felt amazing after spending the earlier part of the day baking in the heat. The recruit who had fainted quickly recovered and didn't remember anything between getting off the bus and waking up in a hard plastic chair.

We spent the rest of the afternoon filling out paperwork before meeting our assigned Drill Sergeants who would take us through the rest of the training. The first order of business was settling into our barracks. We all walked into the barracks clueless, without any sense of order or quiet. The instructors just watched us walk in with disgusted looks on their faces. As soon as we settled into our chosen bunks, they came in screaming for us to pack up all our things and line back up outside. Apparently, they had never seen anything like us before. We were ordered to go back into the barracks silently and quickly, and then stand by our bunks holding our luggage. This drill was repeated five more times. By the last time, I'd noticed it was a quarter to five and was worried we would drill right through dinner. Mercifully, they stopped there and allowed us ten minutes to organize our belongings and line up back outside to march to the mess hall.

There were twenty recruits in my barracks, but at 1655 only nineteen were lined up outside. Two minutes later, the twentieth ran out and got in line. One Drill Sergeant pulled him aside and had him stand at attention while they ordered the rest of us to do push-ups. One hour later, we marched to the main hall for an orientation session, missing dinner entirely. The instructors assured us we would not eat until we learned how to function as a cohesive unit, which we all understood to mean that we had to simultaneously move to and arrive at where we were ordered as a group.

Lights out was at 2100, but we arrived back at the barracks a full hour before, so we finally had some free time to ourselves. My bunkmate was Kevin Smith, who happened to be the fainting guy. Kevin was from Georgia, which made it all the stranger that he would be the one to pass out from the heat. He insisted that it was the first time that sort of thing had happened to him. Next door to us were Jack and Tony, from Maine and Nebraska, respectively. There was also George, who designated himself the barrack bully and clown. A few minutes after lights out, he loudly whispered, "Hey ladies, don't sleep too heavily or you won't see me coming to cornhole you." George was not too bright.

We weren't alone in our barracks, since the drill instructor who ordered us to our bunks and turned out the lights never left. He was assigned to spend the night in a smaller room adjacent to the larger area holding our bunks. Thankfully, we weren't subject to group punishment right then. George was pulled out of the room and brought outside. I don't know what happened to him, but at 0430 when the alarm (Drill Sergeants yelling) went off, he walked back in a dirty mess and headed straight for the showers. He gave us a little thumbs up to show he had not been broken.

At 0500, we started our training, which consisted of a lot of push-ups, sit-ups, and running. Our instructors insisted this was the result of not knowing how to keep quiet after lights out, clumsily trying to link George's behavior to the hard workout. I had my doubts that that was the real reason, however. This was our fate, regardless of what we did or didn't do the night before. Finally, at 0900 we got to eat. The instructors warned us not to eat too much, but I was starving, so I piled my plate high with eggs, potatoes, toast, and sausages. After the last few days of traveling and the start of my training, food had never tasted so good. I wasn't alone in gorging myself; there were recruits from many different units there, and I didn't see one plate leave the chow line not piled high.

Despite our instructor's warning about overeating, we didn't have anything to worry about. After breakfast, we finished our processing, which was mostly filling out more paperwork, getting shots, and getting my head shaved. By the time we went out to complete a pre-lunch run and dressing down, my food was fully digested. I was a runner before coming here so that part of the training was easy for me. Kevin may have been telling the truth about his fainting being a one-off, since he easily kept up next to me in the heat.

George was having a worse time of it. He was very big and muscular, which wasn't the most efficient physique for running in the heat. I had a feeling he spent a lot more time lifting weights than doing cardio. He kept lagging, resulting in the whole group having to slow down so we wouldn't get too far ahead of him. He had one drill instructor run with him, and the instructor's cardio was so good, that he could run beside George while continuously yelling at him.

After we finished the run, one of the other recruits, nicknamed Tebo, told George he ran slower than his legless grandpa. George just responded that we pussies didn't finish too far ahead of him, not acknowledging that we were forced to slow down to keep his pace. He then challenged anyone of us who dared to fight him right there and then. I expected his insolence to drive the drill instructors into a frenzy, but the chief instructor just smiled and said we would get to fight soon enough. The instructor hated weakness but condoned violent talk, as long as you could back it up.

It was the third day when we took our fitness test to determine if we could continue with the training. I had no idea what the test involved, so I was nervous. I had nowhere else to go if I flunked out of basic training. I didn't need to worry, though, since the fitness test was just more of what we had already been doing. I had to do two minutes of push-ups, two minutes of sit-ups, and then a two-mile run. A few of the recruits struggled, but all twenty of us passed, though our Drill Sergeant let us know that we were his lowest-scoring group, and that he was going to correct that.

After the test, we received our uniforms, so now we performed all our activities in uniform, including heavy boots. By the second week, we had started training that

75

didn't only involve standing at attention, running, crawling, and strengthening. They taught us what it meant to be a soldier and the values they maintained. On command, we had to recite the core values from memory. By the third week, we were learning how to fight hand-to-hand and care for our M16s; we didn't use them or have bullets yet.

We got to start fight training mid-morning after a round of fitness training, and nobody was happier about this than George. Since he was the biggest, he'd continually struggled with the running, crawling, and climbing parts of our training, but apparently, now it was his turn to kick ass. Our first introduction to combat was to put on padding, pair up, and whack each other with padded polls until one of the pair landed on their ass or tapped out. The instructor paired up Tebo and George first. Tebo gave it his best and didn't embarrass himself, but it only took around a minute for George to knock him to the ground.

For my first match, I was paired with Tony, who was bigger than me; everyone in my platoon was bigger than me. I decided that my best chance of winning was to avoid direct contact and use my advantage in overall fitness to jab at my opponent and then move away. This worked well. I did take a few big hits, but after two minutes of trying to land a knockout blow, Tony started getting tired. After three minutes, he couldn't hold up his poll anymore, and I just jabbed him in the head and body with the end of my poll until he went down. My Drill Sergeant raised my hand in victory while telling me I fought like a pussy. He left me in the ring to fight again.

The second match against Jackson went like the first for a couple of minutes, but then I was beaten at my own game. Jackson was in pretty good shape too and a much better fighter, so after a while, I was breathing heavily, and the poll felt like a lead weight in my arms. No longer able to defend myself, I went down after a hard blow to the head. The Drill Sergeant just smiled at me and told me to get my ass back in line. Thankfully, I only had to cheer my fellow recruits on and not fight again that day.

George was overconfident and cocky before we started fight training, but now that he'd found something he was better than the rest of us at, he was incorrigible. It wasn't just that he talked tough, he would also randomly bop other recruits on the side of the head and elbow you in the ribs when passing by. The drill sergeants did nothing to stop this. When George tripped Kevin during a run, Kevin face-planted and came up with a bloody lip and nose. The instructor disciplined Kevin for being clumsy. Kevin made the mistake of telling the instructor that George had tripped him, which led to him spending lunch doing sit-ups and push-ups. At this point, we knew the instructors expected us to handle the situation ourselves.

Later that day at dinner, Jack, Tony, Kevin, and a few other recruits decided we were going to teach George a lesson. Over the next week, we formulated our plan and let some other recruits from our platoon, who were also victims of George's antics, in on it. We decided we could not do anything too extreme that could badly injure George, as it had been drilled into us that we were responsible for each other in all areas of training, so pushing him off a raised platform was off the table. Nobody wanted to get kicked out of the army for assaulting a fellow recruit or sent to jail if he broke his neck and died. Thinking about dropping him to his death did bring smiles to our faces, though, so it was a morale boost.

The idea we came up with was not original or very imaginative, but it was a classic and simple to carry out. We also decided to give him a warning first and a chance to change his ways. We didn't expect him to heed our warning, but we wanted to make sure that when we struck, there was no doubt that he was suffering the consequences of his actions. Our plan was to simply spike his drink with laxatives during lunch, the day we were scheduled for more rounds of hand-to-hand combat with the padded polls. As expected, when we told George he needed to stop hitting us, he just called us pussy whiners.

George considered Tebo a friend and always sat next to him at lunch, so Tebo would be the one to spike his drink. That day, Tebo sat at our table with all the recruits who were in on the plan. We swore to each other that we would not rat each other out, even if that meant expulsion from basic training. Tebo had to be sure he wouldn't take the fall if the drill sergeants investigated. That part of the plan went smoothly. Jack sat on one side of George and called him a pussy. George being George, immediately got into Jack's face and laid all kinds of threats on him. While threatening Jack, Tebo leisurely poured a triple dose of Milk of Magnesia into his lemonade and even gave it a little stir.

After Tebo finished, Jack started apologizing to George and promised never to disrespect him again. That eventually mollified George, so he turned back to his meal. Time was running short, so he quickly stuffed his burger and fries into his face and then chugged the lemonade. I worried a little when he seemed to notice something was off in his mouth after drinking the lemonade, but then he just polished off the rest of his fries without saying anything about it.

After lunch, our instructors warmed us up with a two-mile run and some other conditioning. Then we reported to the combat ring to pair off to fight. Fortunately, George had to wait a while before his turn. As the afternoon progressed, he was fidgeting more and more, and his face was tightened up into a grimace. By the time he was called to fight Jackson, he was tensing up his whole body. Jackson was in on the plan, and from the smile on his face, he had his own plan.

Jackson decided to start the fight by feigning attacks and backing off. Just like when I did that the first day, the instructors were not impressed. They wanted us to just get in there and beat each other senseless, even if it didn't make strategic sense. I think the fighting was more entertainment for them than actual training to make us better fighters. George was squeezing his cheeks so hard he could barely move, let alone get a hard strike in on Jackson. Jackson just went for it and slammed the end of his pole right into George's gut.

The effect was immediate and explosive. What I first noticed was the sound of his gut emptying of gas as he bent over and fell face-first into the ground with his ass up in the air. That position allowed the discharge to run down his leg and leak out the bottom of his boots. The worst part was the smell. One recruit in the circle puked up his entire lunch right then and there. The five drill sergeants that were administering the training immediately went into action. Three of them went around and yelled at us to stand at attention around the ring. We were ordered not to move even a muscle. Jackson had it the worst since he had to stand at attention within three feet of George, whose lower half was now wet with excrement.

Two drill sergeants who were disciplining George only lasted a minute before they couldn't stand the smell either. They backed away and ordered Jackson and another recruit named Jason (not privy to the plan) to help George up and walk him to medical. Jackson, Jason, and George led our group while the rest of us marched three abreast behind them. It took us a full half hour to get back to the main base and drop George off at medical. The whole time, he was leaking out poop, while we all closely followed behind in his smelly wake.

As soon as George had been dropped off, we did another three-mile round about run to the obstacle course, where we spent the rest of the afternoon split into three groups learning how to negotiate each obstacle. From my point of view, the plan to punish George had gone perfectly, but predictably, we didn't have a chance to celebrate our accomplishments. Just because we had lost George, training didn't stop or even take a short break. We just quietly gave each other knowingly nods and winks to acknowledge our success. The only one not happy about the outcome was Jackson, who had to partially carry George to the infirmary and took some friendly fire, getting some of the excrement on his hands and uniform.

# GERMAN ANGEL

After basic training, I went on to specialize in computer networking and communication systems, spending another year training and working IT at a couple of bases in the states, before transferring to USAG Wiesbaden, Germany.

It was a beautiful autumn day in Wiesbaden. Freddy and I started our run from our Hainerberg apartment building and quickly made our way off the base northeast towards downtown. Our running loop took us on a tour of the historical buildings scattered around the center of town, then back west into the park adjacent to the city, and finally returning south where we started. Staying fit was very important to the units staying in Hainerberg, so there was a lot of pressure to join in if you wanted to have an active social life. I usually did my run with Freddy once a week because, like me, he kept an easy pace and was fine with doing just the minimum. When I was younger, I ran for fun, but in the Army, it was just part of the job.

While not keeping up appearances at Hainerberg, I worked as an IT tech, managing the computers and networks in the various buildings around the base. It was an easy job, so this morning's run was the most demanding part of the day. Sometimes I got annoyed by officers that knew nothing about computers telling me what I should do or blaming me for problems they caused themselves, but I mostly just tried to disassociate and use the tried and true, "Yes, Sir!" whenever needed. If they stopped downloading viruses onto their systems, I might be out of a job.

I was walking toward downtown one morning to get something to eat when, shortly after I left the secured base area, a woman brushed by me as she ran past. She then looked back, bit her bottom lip slightly, and giggled before speeding ahead. Thirty minutes later, I was walking through one of the squares in town when I heard someone on my left saying, "Hi, hi." It was the same woman, sitting at a table eating a sausage roll. She waved me over and asked if I wanted one. Now I was completely confused. The woman may have been the most beautiful person I had ever seen in my life. She had long blond hair, blue eyes, a perfect nose, and a shy smile; she had the face of an angel. She wore a very tight-fitting outfit that didn't leave a lot to the imagination, so I could see that she had a perfect athletic body that was many inches taller than my average body; I assumed she was going to try and sell me something.

After standing there too long staring at her, she finally abandoned her shy smile and ordered me to sit down, handing me a sausage roll with the command, "Eat!" I ate it, and it was pretty good, though I wished I had some mustard. After breaking sausage roll with this mysterious woman, I spoke up.

"Do want something?" I asked.

She raised her eyebrows in a suggestive manner and, with a deep German accent, replied, "I see you run and think you're cute. Maybe we like each other."

"Really?" I said, then quickly caught myself and changed that to, "Maybe we do like each other. My name is Simon."

"My name is Ida, pleased to meet you, Simon," she said as she stuck out her hand for me to shake. "I'm sorry if I may be a bit forward, but I like soldiers. How do you say? Macho man?"

I was no macho man, but I had enough game to not try and correct her. This interaction made no sense, but if this very hot woman liked short American macho man soldiers, that was what I was going to be. She then handed me a piece of paper with her name and phone number on it and gave me another one of those shy, flirty looks. When she got up, she made sure I got a good long look at her rear end, gently swinging side to side as she walked away.

I managed to get through the rest of the day in one piece, though I did have one officer admonish me for walking around with a stupid smile on my face. I think I was in love. As soon as I got back to my apartment building, I knocked on Freddy's door and told him what had happened. Unfortunately, he just tried to burst my bubble.

"I'm sorry, dude, but if what you say about how she looks is true, then she is after something. Did you buy her anything?"

"No, she bought me a sausage roll," I said.

"Well, that's probably coming. Also, you probably haven't been laid in a really long time. Are you sure she was good-looking? Maybe you're so desperate, you're seeing things. Was it even a girl?"

"I wasn't imagining her, and it was a girl. Maybe she just really likes me?" I replied.

"Maybe, but doubtful. Stay alert and don't give her your credit card," Freddy stated. I didn't know if Freddy thought it was doubtful that Ida was pretty or a girl, but I didn't want to think about the latter.

Just like Freddy, I had my doubts about Ida, but now I needed to prove Freddy wrong, so I resolved that it was perfectly reasonable that the hottest woman in Wiesbaden randomly picked me as her macho man. Regardless, I wasn't in her league, so I would try to keep my guard up the next time I saw her, just in case she didn't want me for my looks. It was a full week before I got the nerve to call Ida, but she seemed happy to hear from me and arranged to meet at a café that coming Saturday.

We arranged to meet at 2:30 PM, but I got there ten minutes early and secured a table outside, looking out at the square. She was very punctual, like you would expect from a German, and arrived at exactly 2:30 PM. Ever the gentleman, I got up from my seat to greet her. She quickly came in and gave me a nice big kiss on my right cheek, then leaned back, and with a big smile, told me how happy she was I had called her back. As I was sitting down, I noticed two swarthy young men staring at us from the next table with partially opened mouths. They quickly turned away when they saw me notice them.

I didn't know what to say, so I played it safe and asked her what she liked to eat. For some reason, she responded by raising her eyebrows and giving me another flirty look before saying, "I eat almost anything." Something was definitely off about her, but I was determined to ignore the red flags and continue on with the date.

She ordered the sausage plate, which came with two large bratwursts on top of mashed potatoes and a side of sauerkraut. I ordered the chicken schnitzel, which came with the same sides. Of course, we washed it all down with some Pilsner. I needed to loosen up a little, so I was on my third bottle already, only halfway through finishing my meal. The conversation was fairly normal, with us each asking about where we worked and what we liked to do for fun. This gave me hope that maybe she was normal, and I really just was her type.

Ida reiterated that she really liked soldiers, so she asked me all kinds of questions about where I worked. In reality, I was an IT tech in an Army uniform, not unlike any of the other millions of faceless people who worked in the corporate world, but Ida wanted to be with a soldier, so I embellished my soldiering resume a bit to make it seem like I was also a fighting man. Instead of emphasizing what I did now, I talked about using my M16 and combat training in the field.

All-and-all, the lunch went well, and we made plans to meet again. Ida was having a few friends over to her apartment for dinner a couple of nights later, and she asked me to help her with the cooking and be her date. Since she was bringing friends to our next date, I told her I wanted to bring my friend Freddy. At first, she wasn't too keen on this, but when she saw I was a little taken aback, she agreed to let him come too.

Ida's dinner party was scheduled to start at 8:00 PM, but I arrived alone an hour early to help her cook. She greeted me at the door with a big hug and a kiss and then sat me down on the couch with a glass of wine. I tried to get up and help a couple of times, but she insisted on doing all the cooking herself. I reminded her that I'd come early to help her, but she told me she'd asked me to come early so she could spend more time with me. Despite all my insecurities, I was starting to believe that Ida really did pick me out of the crowd because she was attracted to me.

Alex and Anna were the first guests to arrive, followed by Hein and then Gerda. They were all very friendly to me. Alex asked me if I liked German beer before giving me a full history of Pilsner in Hesse, which was the German state we were located in. He promised to take me to his favorite spots in Frankfurt for a night out without the women. Ida seemed to appear from nowhere, she gave me a kiss on the cheek and said, "Oh, that sounds like fun!"

"Sorry, Ida, just Simon, Hein, and Harold are invited on this outing," Alex told her.

Ida gave us her best pouty face, then smiled and said, "That okay, let's eat."

Just as we all started to gather around the table, Freddy arrived, which was a relief, since I was starting to think he was standing me up. He came with Carol, who was a private assigned to the same housing unit Freddy and I were in. I had seen her around, but Freddy never mentioned he liked her. I guess he didn't want to come to this party solo.

The conversation stayed mostly on light topics, such as the weather and interesting things happening around town and Frankfurt. Ida's friends gave Freddy, Carol, and I lots of suggestions on good bars and restaurants to go to and beautiful parks to visit. At one point, Hein asked Freddy why he chose to come here, and Freddy honestly answered that he had no choice; we were deployed here to help protect Germany from the Soviet Union. This answer seemed to set Alex off.

"Germany does not need protection. Gorbachev is reforming the USSR, so soon they won't be our enemies anymore," Alex said.

"They will only reform because the U.S. is here, and they're scared of us. Reagan is kicking their ass," Freddy proudly stated.

"You Americans are a little full of yourself," Alex responded.

Before the conversation could go any further, Ida broke in and demanded that we stop talking about politics at the table. She insisted that this was a friendly dinner party and admonished Alex for starting the conversation down that particular path. Alex apologized and told us that he was passionate about politics and proposed a toast to his new American friends. We all toasted and made nice, but I could tell Freddy wasn't happy about Alex challenging our country's role in protecting Europe and fighting Russia. Back at the base, we all hated the communists and didn't accept any other point of view.

Ida was a bit of a General herself and was not going to let anybody add gloom to her party. The rest of the night, we just concentrated on drinking, toasting, and other revelry. After the last guest left at 1:00 AM, I stayed and helped Ida clean up. I was hoping that by hanging around, she would ask me to stay the night, but unfortunately, that didn't happen. After the last dish was cleaned, she gave me a big hug and kiss and told me she looked forward to our next date. When Ida rubbed up against me, I felt like I was going to explode right there. I barely managed to keep my cool, told her I looked forward to it, and quickly left before embarrassing myself.

The next day was our run day, so Freddy and I had plenty of time to hang out and talk about the previous night. I asked him if he was seeing Carol now, but he said he had agreed to buy her coffee for the next month to get her to come with him. She had another boyfriend, so she was just looking for a night out and free coffee. He complained that Germans were ungrateful since we were there risking our lives to protect them from the USSR. I said it was just Alex, but he thought every single German should show us gratitude for being there. That night was also the first time Freddy had met Ida in person, so he made sure to let me know that she was way out of my league in the looks department; like I didn't already know that.

Three days after the party, I had my next date with Ida at an Italian restaurant. She told me about her dreams of becoming a schoolteacher one day, but for now, she was content with just working at her administrative job and having fun with her friends. After that, we started seeing each other more frequently, until we were hanging out every weekend and most weeknights.

She was also getting more intimate with me, but it never moved beyond just hugging and kissing. I tried to subtly hint that I wanted to do more, but she would either ignore my overtures completely or give me one of those shy, giggly looks. After four weeks of this, I was starting to get annoyed. All I could think about was sex, but I wasn't getting any. I imagined that after she hugged and kissed me goodbye for the night, she went back to her apartment to be with Alex. She wasn't dating me for free meals because she insisted on paying for half of them, so I thought I might just have crossed into her friend zone.

Freddy thought Ida was just the kind of girl that liked to tease men and told me that I should find somebody else to have sex with on the side or break up with her. He was worried the stress of the situation was killing me and killing our friendship; he was tired of listening to me complain about not getting laid. I was starting to agree with him, but it felt so good being with Ida that I could never get up the nerve to end the relationship or confront her about why she didn't want to have sex with me, even though she told me she loved me; loved me as a friend?

Fortunately, my work gave me the break from the relationship I needed to put things in perspective. I was busy working on updating software on some of the base PCs when Lieutenant Raves, who was my immediate supervisor, came in and told me that I had been assigned to upgrade all the computers and software in the base commander's office. I was to work with a specialist and two other privates to get it done as quickly as possible while Colonel Banks was away for the week.

We had only eight days to complete the upgrade, which was not nearly enough time, but our orders were to finish in the time allotted. This meant I was working eighteen-hour days for the next eight days straight, even pulling a couple of all-nighters in the end. During that time, I didn't see or even talk to Ida, which hurt at first, but after the eight days were up, I felt better. She was the drug I just went cold turkey to get off of, and now I was through the worst of the withdrawal symptoms. I resolved to break up with her for good as soon as my work assignment was finished.

# HONEY TRAP

After the death march to complete the computer upgrades in the Colonel's office, I went back to my usual, much more relaxed schedule. I didn't like confrontation, so I avoided calling Ida to tell her I was free again for a full three days after finishing the upgrade. I'd resolved to break up with her, so I made a date to meet her for lunch at an outdoor café. She asked me to meet her at her apartment beforehand. I knew that would be a bad idea, but when I suggested that we just meet at the café, she replied with a stern, "You meet me at my apartment and take me to café!"

Ida was always the dominant one in our relationship, so I just conceded. If all went well, I would be out of the relationship by day's end anyway. In the hours leading up to my last date with Ida, I hung out with Freddy for his encouragement. He was all for me ending my relationship with Ida and possibly finding a girl more my type, meaning not ten times better looking than I was. He also missed hanging out with me around base, since I was one of the few people he really got along with.

There was a large mirror in the lobby of Ida's building, so when I walked in, I could see what a mess I was. It was a cool day out, but I was bright red and clammy. I decided not to wait until lunch and just break up with her as soon as I got into her apartment. The stress of the situation was almost killing me; I could barely breathe. After standing there for a few minutes to pull myself together, I took a deep breath and walked up the stairs to Ida's apartment.

I knocked on the door, and when Ida opened it, I almost fell on my face as I stumbled into her entryway and tripped on her throw rug. After getting my bearings back, I blurted out, "Ida, I need to tell you something."

She just placed her right index finger over my lips and said, "Shhh, I say something first." I could never say no to Ida, so I just nodded my head and let her continue. "I think I was not fair to you."

"You weren't?"

"Yes, I love you so much that I didn't want to spoil our relationship by having sex with you, but I wanted it so bad and can now see that you did too," she stated sadly.

"You wanted to have sex with me?" I dumbly asked.

"No, I want to have sex with you, now!" She ended that sentence like it was an order. I was used to following orders, and all thought of breaking up with her immediately vanished. I didn't care what the consequences were, I was a young man and had no ability to pass up on this opportunity.

When it was all done, a few minutes later, I was red and clammy for a different reason, and completely in love, and told her so. She said she loved me too and told me how wonderful making love to me was. We were also hungry, so we got up and went to the café as planned and both ordered the sausage plate. Afterward, we went back to her apartment to have sex again, and I wound up staying the night, waking up early to get back to my base housing to shower and get to work on time.

When I saw Freddy, he looked me in the eyes and immediately knew that I was still with Ida. He looked genuinely disappointed.

"You were supposed to break up with her, what happened?" he asked.

"I was ready too, but then she had sex with me. What was I supposed to do? Say no?" I replied.

"Fuck, I guess not. I wouldn't have either, even though I don't like her. This is fucked up. As long as you're just using her for sex, I guess you have to keep seeing her." He then looked at me and could see I wasn't just using Ida for sex. "You still love her?"

"She said she loves me, and now we're doing it. Of course I love her. I think she might be the one," I said.

Freddy finished with, "I don't know. I don't think this will end well."

I knew Freddy was just looking out for my best interests, but I didn't agree. Ida was the love of my life, and I just knew it. I went to bed that night dreaming of our life together and worried about whether we should live in Germany or the U.S., and how I would get my leave from the Army to start my new life with her.

In the weeks that followed, Ida and I saw each other often, and I spent many days and nights in her apartment, in her embrace. True to form, she always set the schedule and told me what to do. I was just happy to be there. One night during pillow talk, I mentioned that I wouldn't be able to see her the next day because I was doing some more work in the Colonel's office. She got more interested and asked me if I got to see the secret files and help with making the plans. I reminded her that I was just a lowly private and wasn't in on any of the Army's plans, since my opinions were inconsequential to the Army. If I tried to give my opinion to an officer, at best he would silence me and at worst throw me in the brig for insubordination.

Ida didn't bring up secret files or Army plans again for the next two weeks, but she started to get more open with me about her thoughts on the U.S. military's presence in Germany. At first, I didn't agree with her, being a red-blooded commie-hating American, but slowly, I started to see her point of view. When I said to her, "Ya, maybe we don't have to be here anymore," she looked so happy and followed up with probably the best sex we had to date. She was training me.

A few weeks later, I found myself at a bar in Frankfurt with Ida, Alex, Hein, and Gerda talking about politics. Now that they knew I was no longer hostile to the idea of the U.S. military leaving Germany, I spent more time with Ida's friends discussing that possibility. They all thought the threat of war with the Soviet Union was over now that Gorbachev was opening the country up and allowing some dissent. Alex insisted that it was only a matter of time before the USSR became a democracy and freed Eastern Europe from its grip. I thought if that happened, it would be the result of my country forcing it to happen, but they didn't agree.

One afternoon during a pillow talk session, Ida asked me if I could do her a favor, to which I agreed without hesitation before knowing what the favor was. She asked me if the next time I was in the Colonel's office, and had access to secret papers, I could take them and give them to her. My heart sank and I felt a warm tingly sensation in my face; I was speechless since she was asking me to commit espionage against my country.

"It's not what you think. Just something that we can print to embarrass the German government, so they think having foreign troops hosted here isn't worth the trouble anymore," Ida assured me.

"You are asking me to do something that could get me sent to prison for the rest of my life," I said.

"Only I would know, and I love you. I'll make sure you don't get hurt." I didn't respond, so after a moment, she continued, "Don't worry. It was just an idea. You don't have to get me secret papers."

I walked home with what Ida just asked me to do weighing heavily on my conscience. The right thing to do was to immediately break it off with Ida and never see or talk to her again. The problem was that I was in love and needed her. I'd already built up a whole fantasy of our future life together. One thing I couldn't do was tell Freddy. My plan was to put this out of my mind and pretend she was just joking around.

Joking or not joking, our relationship started to change after that. Ida complained more, claiming that I needed to treat her better and take her more seriously. We started to have sex much less often. Sometimes we would start, but at the last second, she would pull away and say she wasn't in the mood anymore, leaving me confused.

A couple of weeks later, Ida told me that she still loved me but was uncertain about her feelings for me, which I didn't understand at all. When I told Freddy, he reminded me that she was out of my league looks-wise and was probably starting to realize that the relationship was doomed from the start; Freddy would definitely say that since he wanted us to break up from the start.

Ida's friend Anna also got into it and scolded me one day when I was leaving Ida's building. She told me that Ida was a good person, and I was making her sad by not treating her right. Over a beer, Alex expressed sympathy for me and told me that if I ever wanted things back to the way they were with Ida, I would have to make a big gesture to show I would do anything for her.

One day, at Ida's apartment, she was being particularly cold towards me. I said, "You seem angry at me. Is there anything I can do to fix things between us?"

"I just want to know you have my back, and I'm not sure that you do," she replied.

"I love you and always have your back," I claimed.

"You made me look bad to all my friends."

"How did I do that? I didn't do anything," I replied defensively.

"I asked you to do something that was very important to me, and you refused and were mean to me about it."

I racked my mind for a second since it had been a month since Ida had asked me to steal secrets for her, but that was the only thing I could come up with that she might be referring to. "Is this about stealing papers from the Colonel's office?"

"It is about supporting me. You can't have a relationship if one partner doesn't care about what is important to the other," she claimed.

I was in a very bad place at that moment. I wasn't going to commit espionage, but I could not bear the thought of losing Ida, since I was convinced that she was my soul mate. My short-term solution was to say, "I'll see what I can do." That immediately cheered her up, and she responded by taking off her clothes and telling me that we would have sex now. This is what I ultimately wanted, so I was happy to follow her orders again.

A week went by, and it was like old times with Ida after telling her I would see what I could do, but then she started sending me signals that I was on a deadline for getting the deal done. She started asking me if I really loved her, and when I said yes, she would respond by telling me she wasn't so sure. She also started to withhold sex again. I was racking my brain trying to figure out how to solve this problem without spending the rest of my life in prison or becoming a fugitive.

One of my favorite sandwich shops was across the street from the Wiesbaden Union Bank. I was sitting on a bench eating my bratwurst bosna, when I noticed a bank employee in slacks and a nice dress suit dumping papers in the large garbage container off in an alley to the side of the bank. I immediately had the solution to my problem.

The next morning, around 3:00 AM, when the streets were quiet, I came back to the bank. I snuck around the side and into the alley, opened up the garbage container, and started looking around. If I was caught, my plan was to just claim I was throwing away some of my own garbage and quickly leave the area while apologizing profusely. Near the top of the pile, I spotted a large binder filled with documents. I didn't want to spend any more time back there, so I just took the binder and ran back to my apartment as fast as I could. If the documents turned out to be useless, I could go back and try again the next day.

Back in my apartment, I quickly realized that I had what I needed to satisfy Ida. The papers showed accounting transactions and metrics with a company called Toryco Inc. Ideally, I would have studied the documents more carefully, but I was tired, and after looking through the first few documents, I got bored. I transferred the contents of the binder to a large manila folder and wrote top secret on both sides in big red letters.

Later that evening, I went over to Ida's apartment. Pretending to be nervous, I handed her the folder, telling her I'd swiped it from the colonel's filing cabinet. She pulled out the documents, did a cursory look over them, and did a little jump for joy. She then gave me a big hug and a kiss. She told me I had better go while she got the documents to people who knew how to use them. I asked her if we could have sex before I left, but she said it was too dangerous for me to stay right then, so I should leave as soon as possible. This was obviously very disappointing, I felt a flash of anger, since I thought giving her what she wanted would result in at least a quickie.

A few days passed since I'd handed Ida the fake top-secret documents and whenever I called to ask her if we could get together, she rebuffed me. I started to wonder if she would dump me now that she'd gotten what she needed.

I irrationally put those thoughts aside and just assumed she was busy doing whatever she needed to do with the files.

Five days after I handed Ida the documents, a long article was published in one of the far-left socialist newspapers published in Frankfurt detailing the United States Army's illegal dealings with Toryco Inc. According to the article, Colonel Banks was running a scheme sanctioned by Army brass and German authorities to bribe German officials, with the goal of maintaining U.S. military presence in Germany. The accounting figures in the documents I gave Ida were evidence that the Wiesbaden Army Garrison was selling military equipment on the black market to generate money to bribe officials, and Toryco Inc. was a company set up to launder that money.

I immediately felt sick to the stomach and my mouth started filling with saliva, and then ran into the bathroom to throw up in the toilet. The article mentioned Colonel Banks by name and implicated my host base in an elaborate scheme to bribe German politicians. Unless I really had randomly grabbed a binder from a garbage container outside of a bank that contained details of U.S. Army wrongdoing, everything in that article was bullshit. Knowing the documents that the article was based on were fake, which therefore made the entire news article fake, didn't make me feel much better. I knew that if it ever got back that I was the source of the fake information, I would be dishonorably discharged at best, and potentially face much worse consequences since Colonels did not like to be embarrassed.

Over the next couple of days, it got even worse. The mainstream media picked up the story and there were demands that the German government open up a full-scale investigation into the U.S. Army's practices. The Army refused to comment. I tried to call Ida, but she said we had to stay underground to prevent the authorities from discovering the source of the leak and told me we could no longer see each other. This was a disaster. The only reason I'd agreed to steal secret documents for her was to make her happy, so she would want to stay in the relationship with me. Now I had no girlfriend and faced the possibility of life in prison without parole. Strangely, my next thought was anger at Ida, not for putting me in this position, but for not having sex with me one last time after I'd handed her the documents; this was all for nothing.

The next evening, on one of the mainstream television newscasts, the news anchor interviewed the President of the Wiesbaden Union Bank. After introductions, they started discussing the scheme involving the Army and Toryco Inc.

"Mr. Schmidt, what can you tell us about Toryco and its dealings with the U.S. Army?" the news anchor asked.

"Well, Karl, I can tell you there are no dealings between Toryco and the U.S. Army. In fact, there is no Toryco Inc.," Mr. Schmidt answered.

"There is no Toryco Incorporated? Can you please further explain yourself, Mr. Schmidt?"

"Of course, Karl. As part of the rigorous compliance training that all of our employees must complete before they start working for us, and periodically throughout the year, I might add, we create scenarios to simulate different situations employees might find themselves in so they can learn how to act accordingly. As part of the simulations, we created a pretend company called Toryco Inc., which is the bogeyman in all our scenarios. All the facts and figures stated in the original article accusing the German government and the U.S. Army of being behind some so-called weapons for bribery schemes are invented to guide our employees' training. I would also like to point out that nowhere in our training documents do we create scenarios that involve selling weapons, though we do talk about what constitutes a bribe of a government official, so that our employees know what to look for."

"That's very interesting, Mr. Schmidt. So, if what you are saying is true, the documents the original article claimed were based on, did not come from Colonel Banks' office, but from your bank?" Karl pointed out.

"Yes, this has nothing to do with Colonel Banks or the U.S. Army. Truthfully, this is quite embarrassing for me. We highly value the privacy of our clients, so we have a system in place to secure or destroy any documents containing customer information. Unfortunately, we never thought it would be necessary to have a process for securing our bank's training material. We have already corrected this oversight. Our own investigation leads us to believe that the material was obtained by someone going through the dumpster in the alleyway beside the bank."

The interview continued like this for a few more minutes and finished with a promise to work with authorities to get to the bottom of how this happened and who was responsible. In the days that followed, the police confirmed that the information printed in the left-wing paper came from the Wiesbaden Union Bank's training material. There were some people that still believed what they originally read, and thought the government was making up the story about the data coming from bank training material to cover up the crime. Eventually, the paper admitted to being duped and issued an apology.

I was a nervous wreck, expecting the military police to come and take me away. As the days and then weeks went by, I started to relax a little, assuming that if something were going to happen, it would have happened soon after the incident. It was always in the back of my mind that I could be found out, so I lived with a constant low level of stress.

One day, several months later, I was walking in the park adjacent to downtown Wiesbaden and saw Ida sitting on a bench. When she saw me approach her, all the love and happiness that she used to convey was replaced by a look of hatred and anger.

"What are you doing here? I don't want to talk to you," she said as I approached the bench.

"Wait, why are you angry? I'm the one who was used and took all the risks. I could have gone to jail," I said.

"You made a fool of me and lied to me, but don't worry, when the police questioned me, I didn't say anything. You can go."

"The police questioned you?" I asked.

"Go now before I scream." She said that coolly with a look of disgust on her face, with a wrinkled nose and upper teeth exposed, like she was talking to a walking shit.

With that, I left and never spoke to Ida or saw her again. I thought I was the one who was wronged, risking my life. Now that I knew Ida had kept my identity secret, I felt more relaxed and decided I couldn't keep what happened to myself any longer.

Over a beer in an Irish Pub, I told Freddy what had happened. At first, he just looked at me wide-mouthed and said he wished I hadn't told him, but then he burst out laughing. He didn't like the fact that he now knew a secret that could get him kicked out of the Army if he didn't report it, but thought it was worth it because it was such a great story. He never thought I should have been with Ida and suspected she was using me for something, so this story just confirmed what he already thought. It also made me look particularly pathetic, which made it incredibly funny.

A few weeks later, I was able to put this whole chapter of my life completely behind me. They were transferring me back to the U.S. After the plane took off and I was safely out of German airspace, I told myself that I had gotten away with it and was free. In reality, it didn't matter where I was located in the world, if Colonel Banks ever discovered I was behind the scandal, it would be the end of me. I had to stay positive and move on for my own health and well-being, so I just pretended it was all over.

# DESERT SHIELD

Captain Briggs came into the room and yelled for attention. I quickly stood up, but not before banging my head on the desk I was under. This brought a smile to Captain Briggs' face. This was his way of having a little fun. "Sir, I'll be done hooking up all the equipment by the end of the day," I reported.

He replied, "I know you will, Specialist, I'll just need my desk for a few moments to get some papers. Feel free to carry on with what you were doing."

"Yes, Sir," I replied, then got back under the desk to finish organizing the cables I was laying out as part of upgrading the computer network in the legal office. After Wiesbaden, I did some short stints at several other Army bases around the U.S., but for the last year, I'd been at Fort Lewis, managing the base networking infrastructure and computer equipment. Much of my time was spent dealing with pissed-off officers with locked-up computers or undoing some damage they did to their own systems. Thankfully, I was dealing with fewer computer viruses than I used to, now that the base had installed software to block access to porno sites.

After Captain Briggs left, I finished up my work and headed outside to enjoy the nice early August weather. I was a little loose with my definition of "end of the day." My work was finished, and it was only 1500, so I had the rest of the day to relax. If I'd told the Captain that I was finished, he would have undoubtedly found something else to occupy my time. Someday, my little fibs would come back to bite me in the ass, but I knew Captain Briggs was in meetings on the other side of the base all day, so that day was not going to be today.

My first stop was the mess hall to get a little snack. It was unusually crowded for mid-afternoon. When I entered, everybody had their eyes glued to the TV watching CNN. Saddam Hussein had made good on his threats and invaded Kuwait. My friend Roy came over to me and said, "You know, this means we're going to war."

"I'm not so sure, why do we care that much about Kuwait?"

"Where do you think we get our oil from? We can't have Iraq controlling all the oil in the Middle East."

"You're probably right," I replied.

Roy proved correct. Two weeks later, I had my orders and was shipped to Iraq to support building new bases of operation in Saudi Arabia as part of Operation Desert Shield. They needed IT specialists to help build up the computer and communication systems needed to manage the influx of soldiers that would be flowing into the country. I started my deployment at Eskan Village Air Force Base, which I and a whole cadre of other IT specialists were assigned to, so we could create the computer and networking infrastructure for the base. Unlike the laid-back atmosphere back in the States, we needed to get the base information systems up and running very quickly, which meant no early afternoons off. My day was scheduled from 0600 to 2000 every day.

I was also on call twenty-four hours a day, which kept me busy most nights. I was running on caffeine and amphetamines.

Each component of the overall system was assigned a set of IT specialists and privates to carry out the task. An officer oversaw the work, and I suppose there must have been a group of eggheads designing the whole thing. My job as the IT specialist was to direct other soldiers to do the back-breaking work of unpacking and placing the equipment where it needed to go. I would then connect things together and do the software installations. Next, I would help get the soldiers who were assigned to use the equipment up and running before moving on to a new task. The work was non-stop from when I arrived in August until November, when I was reassigned to the field.

In a way, I was too good at my job providing IT support to officers on the base. My contributions were noticed, so when they needed soldiers to sneak into Iraq for reconnaissance missions, I was recommended. I wasn't joining up with the special forces or even expected to operate deep within enemy lines, but I was part of a squad that managed communications for other teams that did the real surveillance. They needed soldiers who were literate in maintaining and operating radio and computer gear.

I trained with my platoon that was assigned to this mission from the start of November to early January. I'd spent many years just working in IT with minimal combat training, so it was a little like being back in basic training. My squad was led by Sergeant James, who we just referred to as Sarge. Sarge was very top-heavy, with a large round head, a narrow, wrinkled forehead, broad shoulders, and thick arms, like he spent hours a day just bench pressing. You knew that if you got punched by those big hands, you would stay punched. Conversely, his skull looked so thick, I think he could withstand many head blows before going down. He was hard-assed and thin-skinned at the same time. He liked to work us like we were recruits back at basic training, but in addition to screaming at us, he would make jokes at our expense to the other Sergeants. However, if somebody dared to turn a joke back on him, he would not take it well. You could almost see the steam coming out of his ears on the side of his big red head. When an officer wasn't around, he referred to the IT specialists in the squad as geeks, while the rest of the squad consisted of soldiers, in his view.

Despite being an asshole, Sarge did get us in shape and ready for the mission. By the time my platoon pushed into Iraq in early January, I was mostly a fighting soldier again. My main responsibility was the computer and communication equipment we took over with us. Our platoon only consisted of two squads, led by Lieutenant Casey and Sergeant James. Lieutenant Casey was like me and was more of an expert in electronic equipment than in leading troops into battle. This was fine since our platoon ending up in a battle would mean something had gone very wrong. That was also why Sarge was assigned to our unit, since he had fought in both Grenada and Panama. Lieutenant Casey offloaded most of the responsibility for keeping us ready for battle and security to Sarge. The Lieutenant managed the real purpose of our mission, which was to act as a communications hub.

Including the Lieutenant, there were four of us geeks, one Sergeant, and nineteen other enlisted ranked soldiers who acted as muscle. All the equipment we brought with us, we carried on our backs. We hiked into our location twenty miles within Iraqi territory in two nights of walking. We had fifteen days' worth of supplies with us, and I didn't know what we would do after those fifteen days were up. We set up all our gear in a single day, so after that, we had very little to do when not on guard duty. Sarge set up security with four groups of two soldiers posted at designated spots to act as lookouts. Only the Lieutenant was spared having to patrol.

Ten days after we set up camp, the bombing campaign started, and we became a lot busier ensuring communications between reconnaissance teams and headquarters went through without interruption. It also answered my question about how we would get resupplied. All the planes flying overhead and the bombs going off obscured supply drops to us in the fog of the war. Between maintaining the communication equipment and working my guard shifts, I only slept four hours a day. After a couple of weeks, I felt like I was in a haze. One day on guard duty, I fell asleep, but was then woken up with a startle when a fighter jet flew overhead. I had been leaning up against my patrol partner, who was also asleep. That fighter jet may have saved my life because two minutes after I woke up, and we properly organized ourselves, two of the enlisted men came over the dune to relieve us. Some piece of equipment wasn't working correctly, and I was needed back at camp. Sarge had poisoned the minds of the enlisted soldiers against us IT specialists, so they would have definitely reported us.

It turned out I didn't need to get caught napping to make trouble for myself. One day, while sitting in the sand eating my lunch with the other two IT specialists, Sarge came by and started chewing us out. He said we did not deserve a food break, since we were lazy and didn't do real soldiering. He then looked me right in the eye and called me a pussy. I should have just kept my mouth shut, but answered his provocation with, "Yes, Sir, flat ass!"

He opened his eyes so wide that they seemed to cover his whole forehead. "What the fuck did you just say?" he demanded menacingly. Then, quicker than I'd ever seen anyone move, he was on me, lifting me up off the ground by my neck with one of his oversized hands. I couldn't breathe and thought he might crush my neck and kill me. After a few seconds, he paused and looked around. He must have thought better of killing me like that in front of witnesses, so he gave me one last smile and let me drop to the ground before walking away.

My compadre Specialist Davis looked at me and asked if I was alright. I just nodded affirmative, since I wasn't sure I could get the words out of my narrowed larynx. "That was really stupid of you," Davis said, stating the obvious. "It was all I could do to keep myself from laughing my head off. That was amazing," he continued. Doug agreed with Davis, and they both gave me high-fives and told me they would help watch my back for the inevitable payback that would be coming to me.

# DESERT STORM

It was an unusually hot day for early February in Iraq. For the moment, Sarge was just getting back at me for the flat-ass comment by making my life miserable in small ways. For example, that morning I'd done my guard shift and wasn't scheduled for another one until late that night. Nevertheless, seeing how hot the day was, Sarge decided his real soldiers would be needed elsewhere and and put me back out on patrol during the hottest part of the day. Extra guard duties had become a recurring theme. Since my main purpose for being in the squad was to maintain the communication network we had set up, I thought Lieutenant Casey would have intervened, but he either didn't notice, didn't care, or maybe he was intimidated by Sarge as well. The result was that my guard duties doubled while my IT responsibilities stayed the same. I was tired to the point of delirium.

To the north was nothing but endless sand and rocks for as far as I could see. The sand where I was patrolling was hard and rocky, but I tried to pretend I was on some nice beach to get my mind through the day. Unfortunately, I couldn't lie down without burning myself. As far as any of us knew, our location was hidden and there were no Iraqis in the area. Our camp was in a big crevasse partway down the hill about one hundred yards south of my patrol area. There were some weeds, but no water. My job was to make sure nobody invaded our crevasse. Until that day, guard duty had always been entirely uneventful, with the only sounds coming from occasional bombs going off in the distance and jets flying by. My guard duty partner, who I called Private Ass behind his back, was lying down with his eyes closed about ten yards from where I was posted. He was one of Sarge's real soldiers.

I heard some scratching noises to my left and saw a head, or more accurately the top of a blue turban pop out of one of those crevasses. I immediately started to panic. I could barely move or breathe, and my bowels started to loosen; I had memories of my first encounter with Red those many years ago. I needed to breathe and get myself together. I clenched because if I'd shit my pants, my only choice would have been to let this person kill me, since I would never have heard the end of it if I'd lived. After a few seconds, I could see it was a kid about my height with what looked like a rusty kitchen knife. I had heard rumors that part of becoming a man in this part of Iraq involved a series of trials, including proving bravery by killing something dangerous. I guess today that was me.

The kid fidgeted nervously, eyebrows raised, and eyes opened wide, but despite his obvious fear, he came at me. As he lifted his knife to jab it into my person, he tripped and somehow ended up on his back beside me. I could not hold back the sickness I felt in my stomach any longer and started vomiting, the bile burning my throat. I expelled the contents of my stomach with such force, that it hurled right into the kid's face. His mouth was open, so he started choking and rubbing his eyes. The smell was awful. I made my move and grabbed the knife he dropped and started banging the handle end of it into the top of his head. I felt possessed and must have hit him a hundred times before I saw the kid's skull was cracked and brains had started to mix in with the puke.

Just then, I looked up to see Sarge and three of the guys staring at me. They started to clap and laugh. Jake said it was the funniest thing he'd ever seen. Sarge said, helpfully, "Maybe next time, use the sharp end of the knife." Private Ass started to say something, but just as he opened his mouth, his head exploded. My guys weren't the only ones watching.

The fight was on. We all quickly flattened our bodies onto the ground and started firing towards where the burst of gunfire that took off Ass's head had come from. The other nineteen men also came out of our bunker to join the fight. The enemies were well covered, so we couldn't easily hit them with gunfire. Casey threw a grenade out in the general direction of where he thought the enemy was and must have scored a direct hit. When the grenade went off, I heard screaming, and they left their cover and started running at us head on. As we mowed them down, we missed more enemies flanking us from the right. At that point, I lost myself in gunfire, blood, and guts. I remember shooting and beating men with rocks. I was out of my mind. My ass was hot, so I probably did shit myself. Then things seemed to quiet down, and I saw an injured deer in one of those rocky crevasses. I was so hungry, I went over and started gnawing on its arm. Then some other soldiers saw me and tried to take my prize. I tried to fight them off, but then I felt some pain in the back of my head, and everything went black.

Things were a blur. I saw shapes and colors come and go. Sometimes a pinch. Strange, muffled noises. I remember a blurry face blowing hot air at me and possibly shouting something. I don't know how long I'd been there, but at some point, everything became clear again, and I was staring wide-eyed at a woman in a nurse's uniform. She had thick, curly, reddish hair cut short and a scrunched-up face with chubby cheeks. Her body looked formless under her white uniform that went all the way down to her ankles. She was kind of wide and short like a bulldog.

She finally noticed that I was staring at her and quickly pressed the call button before coming over to start poking at me. She asked if I could hear her, to which I replied, "Yes." It came out as more of a squeak because there was something rammed down my throat. She told me not to try to talk, which was annoying, coming right after she'd asked me a question. Just then, a doctor and another nurse came in and did some more poking. The doctor told me I was in a hospital, which I'd already figured out for myself. He told me I'd suffered a serious concussion and possibly a psychotic break four months before, during an attack on my outpost. Right then, a uniformed woman came in and handcuffed my left arm to the bed rail. The doctor said it was for my own safety. The officer then left the room, but I still saw her standing at attention right outside the door.

I was starting to notice how I felt, and it was not good. My throat hurt from what I assumed was a feeding tube.

My back and neck were sore. I could barely lift my right arm or move my legs, which made locking me to my bed seem like overkill. The bulldog nurse came over to my bedside. I saw her name tag said Irene. She said, "You've been lying here for a long time and your muscles have atrophied." The doctor looked annoyed that she was talking to me about this, but she didn't seem to care and went on, "Now that you're awake, we'll get you up and moving." The doctor leaned over me and said, "First, let's get that tube out of your nose so you can start eating some real food. You are going to feel a little discomfort." He carefully pulled the tape off that was holding the top of the tube to my face and then gave me a little nod before quickly pulling the tube out. It felt like sandpaper rubbing up through my throat and into my nostrils. Tears would have been coming out of my eyes; except I was still very dehydrated.

The nurse said, "drink this," and then pushed a cup of shaved ice to my lips and dumped some in. It felt good, so after enjoying the first serving, I was able to croak out "more." She dumped some more in, but then put the cup down and told me it was not good to overdo it.

Over the next few days, they introduced me back to food, starting with bland soup and Jell-O. Finally, after three days, I graduated to reconstituted eggs for breakfast, baloney sandwiches and potato chips for lunch, and a dried-out cut of chicken, some wet vegetables, and a slice of bread for dinner. Except for a few grunts from the server, nobody talked to me or told me why I was chained to the bed. I tried to strike up some conversation with Irene when she came in to change my diaper; it was kind of awkward, and she wasn't much of a conversationalist. I gave her points for not even batting an eye at the baloney crap smell. Very professional.

Finally, after six days, a judge advocate with captain stripes and a name tag that said Witherspoon, came into my room to catch me up on what was going on. "Specialist Zane, I presume," said Captain Witherspoon. "Yes," I replied, and then, when he didn't immediately reply, I continued with, "What is going on, why am I handcuffed to the bed, am I going back to Iraq, ...". He put up his hand and told me to stop. "Yes, Sir," I replied, not wanting to push him. Witherspoon started, "As you already know, you've been here for four months after suffering a psychological breakdown on the battlefield during an attack on your unit. During the attack, six men from your detachment were killed before your team finally fought the enemy off. From the reports, you fought bravely and might have even been up for a medal if not for one thing. Your Sergeant, Sergeant James, was gravely injured in the attack, and then some of your comrades found you biting his arm. They claimed you became violent when they tried to stop you, so one of them hit you on the back of the head with his gun. Possibly along with your head injuries from the attack, it exacerbated your concussion and led you to be in a coma for four months."

I just sat there for a second, since this was a lot of information to take in. My first question was, "Is Sarge alright?"

"Yes," he suffered several broken bones, but he is expected to make a full recovery.

116

That led me to my next question, which I asked angrily, "Then why am I handcuffed to this bed?"

The Captain replied, "They were informed you violently attacked your Sergeant so were being overly cautious. I've let them know that you are cleared of any wrongdoing, so after they file through some paperwork, you'll be uncuffed. I also have some other good news."

This whole conversation was making me very depressed, so I perked up a bit. He went on, "You've been awarded the Purple Heart for injuries you received during the attack on your platoon."

I didn't mean to seem ungrateful, but he said I fought bravely, so I had to ask, "Am I up for any other medals?"

"No, Sergeant James and Private Slader (aka "Jake") will both receive Bronze Stars, but they felt your actions at the end of the battle disqualified you from further honors."

"But I was severely concussed…" I stuttered out.

"Yes, well, if you have no more questions, I'll get going. Good luck," he tersely replied.

# PSYCH WARD

A couple of hours later, presumably after they got the paperwork, I was uncuffed and the guard left my doorway. Now that they knew I wasn't a criminal, the nurses and staff relaxed around me and said a few words to me now and then. I wasn't in a good mood, knowing they'd denied me a medal because I bit my Sergeant, while suffering from a traumatic brain injury. It sounded like that little bite was the least of his problems at the time, and I suffered way worse than that with the blow to the back of my already concussed head. I was feeling a little fed up and looking forward to getting a medical discharge.

It wasn't to be. A few days after my talk with Captain Witherspoon, an officer and two hospital staff members came into my room and told me I was being transferred to another hospital with a psychiatric ward and rehab care facilities. I protested that I wasn't a headcase, but the officer looked at me sternly and said, "We have our orders."

I gave him a dejected, "Yes, Sir," and got out of bed.

He continued, "That's more like it. These two gentlemen are going to take you to your transportation."

I gave him another "Yes, Sir," and he quickly left. The orderlies helped me get dressed and wheeled me down to a van that was transporting me and a few other patients to a large VA hospital in Seattle, a few hundred miles away. They were cheerful and asked me questions about what I thought of my stay at their hospital and congratulated me for getting to leave. I just politely replied with some "it was nice" and "thank you" responses.

The van taking three other patients and me was set up like a prison transport, where the driver section was fenced off from where us four patients sat. The gate wasn't locked, so the driver must not have deemed us a threat. It was nice to get outside and away from the hospital. It was a cool, but sunny day and the desert scenery driving through eastern Washington and the mountains on the west side was impressive.

My riding mates were John, Steve, and Richard. John was the most talkative, he seemed manic. He kept switching subjects. He would ask me what I was in for, and before I could answer, he would be off looking at the scenery and saying, "Look at that Hill, Whoa!" Then he would point to a car he liked and start talking about that, and then ask me if I had a car, and then on to the next thing. I stopped trying to answer and just nodded whenever he looked at me for a response. I was just a prop in whatever was playing in his head, so I don't think he cared whether I tried to converse with him or not. Fortunately, his high-energy output wore him out, so after around an hour, he directed his mania inward and eventually fell asleep.

Richard and Steve didn't say much in the first part of the drive, but they opened up a little after John started to settle down. Richard was hit with an IUD that blew part of his lower leg off. They had to amputate below his knee. He was going for rehab at the Seattle VA before going home. Steve and Richard had served in the same unit, but Steve took a bullet to his right femur. They'd repaired the bone, and he was going to Seattle to finish his physical therapy. He planned to get back to his unit after he fully healed.

I told them that I suffered a concussion and was in a coma for four months, but I left out the part about being transferred to a psych unit. We talked about our injuries, our families, and the weather. We also complained about Army bureaucracy and how most of the officers we encountered didn't know squat, unlike us battle-hardened soldiers. We kept it light with lots of small talk and avoided all deeper subjects, like what we'd experienced on the battlefield. None of us wanted to go there.

The five-hour drive went by pretty quickly. John woke up during the latter part of the ride, but just spent the rest of the time in his own head looking out the window, muttering to himself. The three of us just let him be. When we arrived, we had to wait a few minutes before an orderly with a wheelchair showed up to help Richard into the hospital. Steve and I just walked ourselves in; well, Steve limped in. John wouldn't leave the van, so they had to call in for additional staff to sort that out. I was already in the main waiting area before that happened, though.

I was the first to be admitted, so I said my goodbyes as the nurse wheeled me through the double doors and into the bowels of the hospital. Eventually, I made it to my new home, which the nurse needed to use her keycard to access. On the other side of the locked doors was a small lobby with a nurses' station and what looked like a security station with a couple of guys monitoring the ward's cameras. There was also a large rec room to the side and some offices and smaller rooms. Beyond this central meeting point were two hallways, and they brought me down the left hallway, which is where the low-risk patients stayed. The other hallway housed more challenging patients. I noticed there were cameras in the lobby area and the hallway to the right.

Nurse Janice, according to her name tag, stopped around halfway down the hall and said, "This is your new home. Let's get you up out of that chair and settled in." She spoke with a calm voice, like a parent wanting to calm a child. When the staff greeted each other, they also said their "Hellos" and "How you doings" in friendly but subdued tones. I didn't think I was crazy before getting there, but I was definitely in a place where the main goal was not to agitate the lunatics.

Janice walked me in and made sure to greet my new roommate, "Hi Tom, what are you reading there?" Tom just grunted and ignored Nurse Janice. That didn't deter her, so she continued, "I hope you are having a really great day. Now, Simon, Tom has been here for a week now, so I'm sure he'll show you the ropes. There is a button right there on your TV remote to call for help if you need anything." She then gave me a smile and left the room.

As soon as she left, Tom looked up and said, "They're not all like that. If they were, I would have gutted myself days ago."

I replied, "That's good to know," understanding what he meant. He apparently didn't like the idea of being a nutjob any more than I did, and with Nurse Janice, you couldn't get away from it.

"Except for daily therapy, they don't bother us much. The staff spends most of their time tending to the fruits in the A wing," Tom went on. I just replied, "Huh," while he continued, "Dinner starts around six or whenever the meal cart gets here."

That was good because when he mentioned dinner, I realized how hungry I was. All I had eaten that day were a couple of soggy slices of French toast around 11 hours before. So far, all the hospital food had really sucked and there was not nearly enough of it to fill me. Come to think about it, I never got my fill with my unit in Iraq either, so I'd been hungry for a long time. Unfortunately, when the cart arrived, the food was no better than in the last hospital. Just a small dry chicken breast, greasy tater tots, and soggy overcooked vegetables. I did have some bright red Jello to finish the meal off with, however. There were no condiments, but I got a soft spork to eat with and an overly small napkin. The spork was useless with the tough piece of chicken, so I ate that with my hands.

I finished the whole meal in under two minutes and then asked Tom if that was it for food for the day.

"They usually have candy and crackers in the rec room in the evening. At around seven, a lot of us like to go there and play cards. You want to come?"

I sure did. I wasn't much of a card player, but crackers and candy sounded good.

The rec room was already crowded when we showed up at 7:00 PM on the dot. There was one group of patients playing cards at a round table along with a staff member, but around half the men were just sitting by themselves, looking very sad and sedate. Tom noticed me looking at the row of somber patients and said, "The pills really kick in by this time of the day. Don't cause any trouble and you won't end up like them."

We sat down with a group of five other patients sitting by the snack table. They were just talking and looking bored. Dry crackers weren't much of a treat, but I dug in anyway. After my mouth was full to the point where I struggled to swallow, I noticed another patient staring at me menacingly. Even though he was sitting down, I could tell he was big and spent a lot of time lifting heavy things. His jaw was large and square. He looked like a caricature of a soldier; a face they might use in a recruiting commercial for the Soviet Army. His forearms looked as thick as my legs, and he could probably pop my head with those big hands. His hands reminded me of Sergeant James. He got up and walked towards me.

"I don't like you," the big man flatly stated.

I didn't know what I was apologizing for, but quickly said, "Sorry."

"You're going to regret it," he grumbled.

Tom tried to defend me, "He's a good guy, Byron, you don't have to worry about Simon." Tom quickly shut up when a couple of the other guys just looked at him and shook their heads side to side.

I started to shake a little and then looked at Byron and said, "What did I do?"

He ignored my question and menacingly, albeit with a slight smile, said, "Watch your back, don't sleep, don't drop your soap, don't relax. I own you now. Understand?"

Just then, Dave, wearing a blue staff uniform, came by and cheerfully asked how we were all getting along. Byron quickly went from menace to delight, which made him even more scary.

With a big smile and cheery demeanor, he told Dave, "Just getting to know Simon here. I love getting to know the new guys."

"Now you behave yourself, Byron," Dave jokingly said. "Dr. Brown is available to talk to you for a few minutes before he goes home if you would like to ask about that thing we talked about now."

"Absolutely!" Byron got up and gave me a little sinister smile and a wink, and then followed Dave out of the rec room.

"You are so fucked, dude," Jack stated.

"What did I do?"

Bob said, "You didn't do nothing. The guy is a psycho and likes to hurt people. I heard he's here for almost beating a guy in his own unit half to death."

I said, "Shouldn't he be in the brig then?"

"His lawyer convinced a judge he only did it because he was suffering from severe PTSD. You saw how he changed when Dave came up to us. They all think he's charming."

"Was he just fucking with me, or am I really in danger?" I nervously asked.

Bob, Jack, and Tom simultaneously affirmed that I was in real trouble.

I went back to my room to be by myself. I felt nauseous, I was lightheaded, and shaking. My stress level was through the roof. It was like I was a child again worrying about drunk Stepbad, but this was even worse. I didn't have PTSD before entering the psych ward, but I had it after meeting Byron. I barely even remember the attack on my unit. *Why was I here?* I was trapped in this ward, so I just had to find a way to get through it.

Tom came back to the room around an hour later and we watched some TV. Suddenly, things were awkward between us. I think he felt bad for me, but also didn't want to antagonize Byron and make himself a target. He seemed to sleep well, but I was up most of the night. I wished I had some NyQuil.

The next morning, Dr. Brown brought in a guest speaker to talk to us about calming techniques we could all use to lower anxiety. As I walked down the hall, I felt a very sharp pain in the back of my right Achilles and my shoe came off. I looked back right into Byron's big chest, and he smiled back at me, "I'm sorry. I wasn't looking where I was going. You know a lot about being sorry, don't you?"

He walked by me as I stopped to rub the back of my ankle and put my shoe back on. My tormentor had started things off by giving me a flat tire. This was a middle school-level prank, but I suspected it was quickly going to escalate to maximum security prison-level high jinks. Tom waited for me, standing there looking down with pursed lips. He was a good guy and was worried on my behalf, but not brave enough to intervene. I was on my own.

Ted, the guest speaker, gave us lots of good information on breathing techniques and some guided imagery exercises. We closed our eyes and imagined ourselves walking down a quiet path alongside a burbling stream. There were birds softly chirping and a nice cool breeze. Unfortunately, halfway through my walk, Byron showed up, pushed me into the water, and laughed hysterically while taking a piss in my direction. Ted said it takes time to develop these stress-lowering techniques into daily practice. I did have a small moment of happiness when I imagined myself putting a hole in Byron's head with my M9. Unfortunately, that wasn't enough to stop him; this monster didn't need a coherent brain to function.

The rest of the day, I kept watch over Byron's location relative to mine and tried to stay clear. The only time I left my room was to attend my mandatory therapy session with Dr. Sue, who was assigned to my care. If my goal was to convince Dr. Sue to discharge me from psych, I wasn't off to a good start. The lack of sleep and paranoia about what Byron was going to do to me next put me on edge. She told me a lot of patients have trouble adjusting, but with time we would get there. She wasn't in a rush to get me out of there. Apparently, congress had authorized a large increase to the VA mental health budget.

For the next two weeks, Byron laid off me and I started to relax. He would even sometimes give me a hearty, "Hi, Simon," when walking by and pat me on the back. I twinged every time he brought one of his oversized hands by me, but he would just give me a little smile and a wink. I tried to fool myself into thinking he was just putting me on those first couple of days, but in my heart, I knew this was part of a game he was playing with me. Not knowing what was going to happen was making me even more anxious.

Without Byron hanging over me, Jack and Bob relaxed and let me into their friend group. We passed the time playing liar's poker and bullshitting. All three of us liked reading, so we would sit and do that together, followed by discussions about what we read. It passed the time because weekdays only consisted of one or two hours of individual and group therapy and mealtime, plus another hour of rehab to build my strength back up from my time in the coma. Dealing with the boredom was the most challenging part of getting through the week.

A couple of weeks into my treatment, Byron changed tactics again. He moved on from mostly ignoring me, except for the cheerful greetings, to taking me in as his buddy. After my morning therapy session with Dr. Sue, I entered the rec room and started walking over towards Tom, Jack, and Bob, who were sitting by the window already into what looked like a good bull session. They smiled as I approached, and then suddenly, the air was knocked out of my lungs as I felt like I walked into a wall. Byron wrapped me in a side hug and steered me in the opposite direction towards a couple of chairs in the corner of the room. For his size, Byron was as stealthy as a crocodile; I didn't see or hear him until after he had grabbed me. The guys looked concerned as I was led away but didn't try to intervene.

We approached the two most comfortable chairs in the rec room. They were currently occupied, but when they saw Byron approach with me undertow, looking like his bitch, they quickly got up and left without being asked. I didn't know what I was expecting, but it wasn't a charm offensive. He smiled (a friendly smile) and told me to take a seat. "I think we got off on the wrong foot. You seem like a cool guy that I should get to know better," he told me.

"Re-e-eally?" I stuttered.

"Oh ya, my sessions with Dr. Brown have been going really well lately, and I think it's time for me to make a friend."

"You want me to be your friend?" I asked, confused.

"I sure do, Simon. Where did you grow up?"

We talked for almost an hour. He would tell me stories about the guys back in his old unit. By his telling, he was a very popular guy who, along with his cohorts, liked to joke around and kick some enemy ass. For my part, I felt trapped. I really wanted to go hang out with my real friends, but I also didn't want to set Byron off. Despite his friendly demeanor, I knew I was more his prisoner than his guest. I was too on edge to open up to him, but made sure I answered his questions and feigned interest in what he had to say. I was careful not to give him too much information that he could use against me later.

"Look at the time, lunch is a waiting..." Byron said, cheerfully ending our conversation. "Now that we're such good friends, I really look forward to many more interesting discussions with you in the future. You're the best friend I've had in years."

I didn't know how to reply to that, so I just replied with an awkward thank you and let him leave first before getting up and hurrying back to my room. Our meal cart was already there, and Tom had finished his sandwich and chips. He looked up and said, "Man, I thought you might not make it back before they came and picked the food back up."

"I'm sure it wouldn't have gone to waste."

He smiled back and said, "No."

Tom let me eat my lunch, which took me all of three minutes, and then breached the subject of what had just happened with me and Byron. "It looked like the two of you were having a nice discussion," he said warily.

"Something's not right. He told me I'm his best friend and wants to hang out with me every day," I replied. I also updated Tom on some of the other stories Byron told me.

Tom said, "He didn't have any friends in his unit. They were all scared of him, just like they are here. Shit, man, you got to get out of here. This isn't good."

I agreed, but I couldn't get out, unless I wanted to escape and go AWOL from the Army. I didn't go back to the rec room that evening, but instead sat in my bed obsessing about my situation. If Byron's goal was to separate me from my friends, it was working. The only way to stay away from Byron was to stay in my room.

# BYRON

For the next couple of weeks, Byron persisted in being my best friend. I tried to stay in my room, but he would just come in and talk and play buddy-buddy. If Tom was in the room, he would just tell him to leave. I started spending most of my time in the rec room again since I thought it was safer there than being in my room alone with Byron. It got a little weird in the shower with him waiting outside my stall with a towel. I told him that handing me a towel wasn't necessary, but he ominously replied, "The proper response to someone doing you a favor is 'thank you'." I stopped showering.

Dr. Sue started to notice something was up in our sessions. "If you don't mind, I've noticed that you've been increasingly anxious in the last couple of weeks. From my notes, it looked like you were really starting to do better." She then turned up her nose and asked, "Have you been showering?"

"No, I've just been pretty busy," I nervously replied.

"I can tell, but keeping up your hygiene is important. Are you feeling depressed?" She asked me with concern.

"No, No, I'm fine. I'll start showering more often. I just got into a bad routine and ..." I didn't have anything more to say, so I sat silently for a few moments. I could see her looking right through me with a furrowed brow. "It's Byron..." I stopped there.

"I noticed you and Byron seem to be really getting along. You're the first friend he's had in here, and I think you've been a good influence on him. How do you see your friendship with Byron?"

I felt that I was already digging myself into a hole that would keep me in this place for the next hundred years. I didn't want her to think I was paranoid, so I lied, "Yes, it's nice to have a friend. I'll try to keep up with showers and do what you want me to do."

"I just want what is best for you, Simon. You suffered severe trauma and are here to get better, so when you leave here, you'll be able to find some peace, if not happiness. It is important that you do what is best for yourself, not me."

Little did she know, late at night when I was not sleeping, I would think about what was best for me. The night before I had fantasized about driving a broom handle up under Byron's chin and through his brain. The image did give me a moment of happiness. What would Dr. Sue think if I told her that?

"There, you can smile. See, I think we've made some progress today," she stated cluelessly. "It looks like our time is up, so I'll see you on Wednesday morning at 9:00 AM sharp."

I had to get better at working the system if I ever wanted to get out of there. That meant putting on a strong façade around the doctors and keeping up with my daily hygiene. I could time my showers when Byron was in his therapy sessions. Unfortunately, Byron was also adjusting.

After lunch, I walked into the rec room. Fortunately, Byron wasn't around. I spotted Jack and Bob sitting in their usual location and went over to hang out with them. They at first looked a little concerned, looking back and forth to make sure I didn't have Byron in tow. They were just about to start a game of liar's poker, so I joined in. After a while, it seemed like old times. We were playing games and joking around. I could almost forget my troubles.

When I looked up from my dollar bill, I saw both Jack and Bob staring past me a little wide-eyed. This confused me until I felt two oversized hands hit my shoulders. Those hands started massaging me slightly too hard.

"Ahh, look at this. You boys seem to be having so much fun," Byron said as he squeezed my shoulders. "I don't remember being invited to this little get-together. It can't be Simon's fault, he's my best friend, right, Simon?" I couldn't see Byron, but from the look on Jack and Bob's faces, I knew Byron was scaring the shit out of them.

"Nu, Nu, No, I looked for you, but you weren't around, so we just started playing. We're not leaving you out," I said.

Byron ignored me and said "Hey, Jack, you saw me in here earlier and never once asked me to play. You either Bob. You're trying to get between me and Simon. I know what's best for Simon."

Bob replied, "It's not like that, Byron, we weren't planning to play, it just happened. We were just sitting here, and Simon came over to us."

This set Byron off. He let go of me and sat over next to Bob, moving faster than I thought a human was capable of. He kept that creepy contemptuous expression on his face that he used to keep the orderlies and nurses from suspecting any problems, but the growl in his voice conveyed pure animosity. "I take care of my friends, Bob, so how do you think it makes me feel when you blame your mistakes on Simon? I won't tolerate it. There will be consequences. Come on, Simon, you need a real friend right now."

Byron grabbed my arm and walked me over to our usual spot in the corner. After sitting down, it was like the previous couple of minutes had never happened. He happily went on talking about his life like we were besties. He never told me anything meaningful. It was more like bragging about how he was the best at this and that. He was voted captain of his football team, and all the guys in his squad loved him, yada, yada, yada. He was a sociopath, and I was his charge. If I did try and interject, he would scold me for interrupting him. If he thought I wasn't paying attention, he would say something like, "I'm not boring you, am I? I'm pouring my heart out to you, so the least you can do is listen." I had to put all my effort into paying attention and nodding at the right moments. It was exhausting.

The next day, I saw Jack and Bob in the hall walking to group session and went up to them to apologize. They didn't even look at me. Jack said, "Please, just stay away. I'll be out of here soon and don't want any more trouble." As usual, in the session, Byron made me sit next to him in the group circle. I was so upset about my encounter with Jack that I didn't even realize that the counselor mediating the session that day had called on me.

I felt a soft nudge from Byron. I quickly looked at him, and he nodded toward Niome, the counselor. Before I could open my mouth, Byron spoke for me. "I'm sorry Niome, Simon wasn't trying to be rude. He's just having a hard time adjusting to life here. I get really worried about him."

Niome replied, "You sound like a good friend, Byron." She looked at me and continued, "It's okay, Simon, we all have bad days. Would you like to share with the group what is troubling you?"

I mumbled, "No, I'm fine."

"We're all here to help. Part of recovery is opening up and expressing yourself. If you hold it in, that thought or memory troubling you will, as I like to say, rot in your system, and continue to cause you pain and affect your ability to function outside of these walls, so give it try! This is a judgment-free zone." She looked at me with a big smile and eagerly waited for me to spill my guts. I had to say something.

"It's just I haven't been sleeping that well." Apparently, that wasn't enough, since she and half the other ten captives continued to stare at me. She really seemed interested.

"I have nightmares from my time in Iraq, so I don't like to sleep," I lied.

She nodded like she knew exactly what I was talking about. Byron patted me on the shoulder and announced how proud he was of me for opening up. Niome looked at him motheringly, and said, "yes, even a little step is a step." For the last ten minutes of the session, my confession was the focus of her attention. She implored the others to follow my example and let their pain out. I was thoroughly embarrassed, but because I was Byron's chattel, nobody would tease me about this. I was avoided like the plague.

That afternoon, Tom walked into our room. He was obviously concerned and walked straight towards me. "Did you hear what just happened?"

I had been holed up in the room since the group session, so I hadn't heard about anything. "No."

"It's Jack. He was beat up in the bathroom pretty good," Tom said.

"Wait, what happened to Jack?" I replied.

Tom backed up and said, "Luis said he walked into the bathroom and heard a moan from one of the stalls. He went over and asked if he was okay and got no reply. He went out and found Dave, who peeked under the stall and saw it was Jack. Security got the stall door open, and Jack was barely conscious."

I felt all of the energy in my body drain out of me, since I could guess what had happened to Jack, but still asked, "Do you know what happened to him?"

"I don't know. Luis said he looked like maybe his head got stuffed in the toilet and his breathing was raspy, like he couldn't get a breath. They took him out of the ward in a stretcher."

"Anything else? Where was Byron?" I asked.

"I don't know. I think Byron was just sitting in the rec room while all this was happening. You think it was Byron?" Tom asked me.

135

"Yes, he threatened Jack yesterday because he and Bob were playing liar's poker with me. I need to figure out what to do," I said, worried.

"You need to tell a Doctor before Byron kills somebody!" Tom stated.

"I don't have proof. Maybe Jack will tell them?"

"Tell them you heard Byron threaten Jack! Come on, he might come for me next," Tom pleaded.

I didn't like any of this, but I knew if I sat around and thought about it too long, I would lose my nerve. I gave Tom a nod, got out of bed, headed out the door, and walked down the hallway toward the staff's desk to find somebody to report this to. I saw Dave in the lobby and decided to tell him. I called out to him and walked over, "I need to tell you something about what happened to Jack."

Just when I got within a few feet of Dave, I felt that familiar big-handed hug. Byron injected, "Yes, we need to tell you something. What happened to Jack is not acceptable. How can we feel safe if you are letting people into the ward to hurt us? Simon and I are worried sick."

Dave answered, "We don't know what happened yet. I'm not allowed to talk about it other than to suggest you take your concerns to your assigned therapist or Dr. Brown."

Byron answered with false panic, "Dr. Brown is my therapist, and I don't see him around. How are you going to keep us safe?"

Dave didn't have a good answer other than to suggest staying in our rooms until they had more information. I just stood there like an idiot in Byron's grip while Byron gave Dave a disgusted snort and walked me over to our corner of the rec room.

"That wasn't smart, Simon. You don't rat on your friends. Go back to your room now, we'll talk more about this later," he calmly whispered.

He then let go of me. I stumbled out of the rec room and walked quickly back to my room. When I got there, I shut the door, looked at Tom, and told him we were in trouble.

"What do you mean, *we* are in trouble?" Tom angrily replied.

"I tried to tell Dave about him threatening Jack, but Byron got to me first and didn't let me. He's going to do something to me now. I don't know what," I sputtered on.

"Fuck, well, whatever he's going to do, it will be soon. Jack will implicate Byron, so Byron has to get his payback before he talks," Tom stated.

Tom and I both stayed in our room for the rest of the day. Tom skipped his therapy session, but nobody came to remind him. We didn't talk, just read and watched TV. I could not hide out in my room forever, since after a few hours, I had to go to the bathroom. Just when I got to the point where I couldn't wait any longer and started to stand up to go, Byron walked into our room and closed the door behind him. I sat back down, expecting him to threaten us, but he apparently wasn't in the mood for more words.

He went for Tom first and punched him in the throat, rendering him mute. Tom went down to the ground, holding his neck in his hands. He looked like he was choking. Byron then kicked him in the gut and spit on him. He then looked at me. I yelled for help.

My yell wasn't very loud, and I only got a couple of 'helps' in before Byron was on me too. He repeated, "I was your friend, I was your friend..." as he rained blows down on my head and body. After what was likely only a few seconds, security burst into the room and dragged Byron off me. My head was spinning from the blows, but I could see at least four security officers trying to hold Byron down and taking some blows themselves. There was lots of shouting, and Byron did not give up easily. Eventually, a nurse came in and managed to jab a needle into Byron's arm. After another minute or two of struggling, Byron finally passed out and it was over.

After Byron was sedated, and they had dragged him out of the room, doctors and nurses came in and treated both Tom and me. Tom was completely passed out, and I saw them intubate him and wheel him out on a bed; I later learned that Tom's larynx had been fractured. They must have determined my injuries were less severe, so they took me out of the room in a wheelchair and into another room in the main hospital. My diagnosis was a concussion, which concerned the doctor given my previous head injuries, including my four months in a coma. They kept me in the hospital for observation for three days before moving me back to the psych ward. I wasn't happy to be going back, since my three days in the main hospital was the first time in many weeks, I'd been able to truly relax.

I was not popular in the psych ward. Since Byron was no longer around to blame, and he was too scary to confront even if he was, they blamed me for what had happened to Jack and Tom. Bob made it a point to tell me that I'd almost got Jack killed by not standing up to Byron. I didn't notice Bob standing up to Byron either, but I let it slide. I avoided the rec room as much as possible, but when I needed to get out of my room, I hung out at the side with the more demented patients from the A-wing. Only a few of them cared enough about what went on to be antagonistic.

Jack was due for release anyway, so after spending a month recovering from the attack, he was discharged from the hospital and retired from the Army. Tom was back in our room a week after I got back. He was very hoarse and was on a liquid diet, but unlike the other patients, he wasn't angry at me. He was just happy nobody was permanently damaged, and Byron was out of our lives. Byron had been transferred to a psych ward for dangerous and violent lunatics somewhere else in the system.

In the end, I think the events with Byron helped me get out sooner, since my being there was a disruption to the treatment of all the other patients. Everybody in the ward had some type of PTSD, so I had brought the violence they were trying to heal from in therapy back into their lives. Three weeks after I got back to the psych ward, Dr. Sue said I had made enough progress to go home. One day later, I was assigned to a local base while I waited for my full discharge from the Army.

# SoDo, Seattle

In just an hour, it had gone from a nice cloud-covered, cool day to hot and sunny. Even in the summer, I could usually count on cool Seattle mornings, but not today, even though it was only 7:00 AM. I was five miles into a ten-mile run, and my eyes were burning as the sweat poured into them. In the years since I left the service, I'd developed a consistent routine. Every morning, I woke up at six, went for a run, went to work at my IT job, and then came home. The only things that changed were what and where I ate, though most of the time it was chicken and vegetables at home. On the weekend, I'd run ten to twenty miles on Saturday and take Sunday off, and usually go for a long walk around the city instead.

My location in Seattle's SoDo neighborhood was perfect. There were parks in all directions I could run to, but my favorite run, when it was not stormy, was down along Elliot Bay. With some weaving and bobbing to get around urban obstacles, I could run all the way to Discovery Park and back. Sometimes I would go the other way, and cross over the I-90 bridge to Bellevue or even Issaquah. When I got too far from home, I could always take the bus back.

Looking back to when I first left the Army, I continued my therapy at the VA hospital a few blocks from my apartment, as an outpatient. For the first couple of months, I would show up at my weekly appointment and my therapist and I would just say a few polite greetings and then mostly sit in silence for the next hour. For some reason, she didn't press me to open up and spill my guts. We were both okay sitting in awkward silence for an hour. Maybe it was a nice break for her after dealing with more challenging patients.

During one of the sessions, she broke the silence by asking me what made me happy. After shaking myself out of my relaxed stupor, I intelligently answered, "I don't know."

"Does coming to your sessions make you happy?" she asked.

I thought maybe she was angling to end our therapy sessions. "I guess so, it's nice to have a little quiet time; why do you ask?"

"I'm glad you feel you can relax here, and it's been nice to get a little break in my day too, but now we have to start making some progress so you can go out on your own."

I was right! She was using my session to catch up on downtime, but unfortunately, she was now looking to dump me. Her bosses were probably looking to increase patient turnover, since there were always more soldiers coming back from the war who needed help.

She went on, "So, what makes you happy? Any answer is a good one. Something you do or experience or think about. Anything?"

"Weeelllll, I like eating."

"Anything in particular?"

"Hamburgers!" I exclaimed.

"Good, hamburgers make you happy. Anything else? Not food related. If nothing now, maybe something you used to do?" she managed to say without a hint of condescension.

The first thing that came to mind was killing people, but that was too dark and might get me put back in psych lockup. Firing my weapon when I was in the Army did make me happy, though. Instead, I said, "Running. Before I joined the Army, I was a long-distance runner."

"Why did you stop running?"

"I had to run a lot in the Army, but since I was discharged, I just walk to and from work and then go home and watch the TV until bed," I answered.

"Yes, but why don't you run for fun anymore?"

"I have no idea; I just don't."

"Think harder," she pressed me, "when was the last time you ran for fun?"

I immediately knew the answer to that question but waited a few minutes to speak. "My last fun run was with my best friend Jose, a few days before I joined the Army. I joined the Army because he died in an accident." She got me. I hadn't thought of the accident or Jose in years. I'd joined the Army to get away from that, and now I was back in that moment, and tightening up my whole body to keep from crying. She promised that we would dive into those feelings more deeply in our next sessions, but she wanted me to go for at least one run before that.

The next day, I went for a two-mile run, which was the first time I had run on my own volition since joining the service. Within a month, I was running every day and out of (or fired from) therapy. It could have been that I'd stopped running for myself because it reminded me of Jose or because it was something I was compelled to do for many years, but whatever the reason, I was a recreational runner again. I can't say the act of running was fun or made me happy, but I felt better in general during the rest of the day.

I thought about joining a running club or asking someone at work if they wanted to run with me, but decided that I didn't want to try and recreate the comradery I'd had running with the PRC when I was younger. For now, it was just something solitary I did for myself.

# PROTEST

Somewhere in the back of my consciousness, I heard, "Hey, Sauce, Sauce, Saauuusssee!" I was then stunned back into attention by a hard object hitting me in the head.

"What, what, did something happen?" I said while waking back up.

"Yes, Sauce, you fell asleep. We're discussing important things that you are involved in, so please try and pay attention," Dagger said. Despite calling himself Dagger, Dagger was the cleanest-cut person in the room. He always wore beige khakis and a poplin button-down dress shirt; the best the Gap had to offer. Dagger was our leader, so he must have felt dressing nicely gave him some legitimacy. In his defense, even though none of the slobs in the room cared how anyone dressed, Dagger was the face of our movement. Maybe the suburban moms that saw him interviewed on the local newscasts were more comfortable hearing his radical bullshit dressed up in khakis. Dagger's public persona was called Ken Johnson, which I assumed was his real name, though he may have picked it to match his wardrobe.

"Sorry, I had to get to work early today, so it's been a long day," I said. My day job was still working in IT at a local Seattle company. My second job, as a member of the SNOE (Socialism Now Or Else) organization, was my night job. Tonight, we had our weekly meeting, which started at 8:00 PM; it was now 1:00 AM, and I was exhausted. Not only was I exhausted, but these meetings were mind-numbingly boring. Instead of just getting to the important stuff, like what windows we were going to break or roadways we would block that weekend, people just went down into endless rabbit holes. For instance, there was a three-hour argument about whether this week's leads should champion feminists for corporate abolition, or we should lead with anti-Jesus slogans. The leads referred to the people holding signs out in front of the march. They would get the most coverage.

Abolishing corporations was closer to our socialistic ideals; therefore, it made a lot of sense for us to make that our main message. On the other hand, holding up signs protesting and denigrating Jesus generated a lot more attention and press coverage. We would get the initial coverage from local news when they came out to see why we were blocking traffic, but the national media would also pick it up. There would be countless numbers of talking heads from the religious right condemning our actions. In the end, making people angry and getting maximum press coverage was really what SNOE was all about. There were over fifty core members of SNOE, and I'm sure there were some true socialists who wanted to do away with capitalism, but most of the core members were just young people who liked to cause trouble, break shit, and get laid. In the end, we decided to block Fifth Avenue in downtown Seattle that Friday at 5:00 PM, to protest Jesus.

145

At 4:30 PM on Friday, we started staging. We didn't just want to mill around our target location of Fifth and Pine and jump out into the street at 5:00 PM sharp. We would gather in small groups within a four-block radius of the target with our signs hidden away. At 4:55 PM, all of the small groups would then quickly converge on the target location and be out in the street approximately five minutes later. We would then unveil our multitude of signs demanding the end of corporations, women's rights, gay rights, Native American rights, all kinds of profane anti-police rhetoric, and our antireligious signs out in front as planned. It went off smoothly. By the time we had all converged, we had a healthy-sized group of around thirty supporters standing in the middle of the road blocking angry commuters. If we could hold our phalanx for more than half an hour, we could expect our numbers to at least double. Seattle was full of young people looking for a good protest to boost their adrenaline.

I always made sure I stood in the middle of the group so I could hide in the chaos. I never held up a sign either, telling my comrades that I preferred to hold my fist up and shout, like Lenin. "This is fucking awesome! We'll show the pigs what we're about tonight," Deuce said to me.

"You bet you we will!" I shouted back.

"The pigs really got here quick, man. I was hoping we could march down the block a little before they started setting up blockades," Deuce complained.

"They're omnipresent," I said.

"No, I think we have a rat that tells them our plans. When I find him, I'll kill him."

"How do you know it's a guy," I asked.

"Rats are guys," Deuce said confidently.

We had been on the road for more than an hour, and it seemed like the number of protesters had swelled to hundreds of people. I saw a lot of drinking, and many of the newcomers had covered their faces with bandanas. Protesters started throwing objects at the cops; I could feel it getting out of control, so I had to safely and discreetly make my exit from the crowd before things got uglier. With all the people and pandemonium, I was able to slip out of the group without any of my SNOE comrades noticing. I was dressed like some geek just trying to get home after work, so by walking at a normal pace with a slight look of fear on my face, the cops let me slide out of the combat zone. As soon as I was free, I beelined it to a burger joint a few blocks away and then home. Protesting makes me very hungry.

Despite the cops boxing us in on Fifth between Pine and Olive Way, SNOE had a very successful night. All of the local news organizations had sent reporters to cover us. There was even a helicopter. When the police finally moved in to disperse the crowd, all hell broke loose, and protestors smashed the windows of several businesses. I made my exit from the crowd long before it devolved into a riot. I didn't want to be arrested. The signs disparaging Jesus also had the intended effect. Our little event made the national Sunday news rounds.

The next day, I had my usual debrief with Kevin Smith, my former bunkmate from basic training. We were never stationed together after basic, but we kept in touch. After Desert Storm, he spent a year stationed at Fort Lewis before retiring from the service and joining the Seattle Police Department. Kevin was very ambitious. He wanted to become a detective and move up the ranks from there. Unlike me, he had a plan for his future.

Like most cops, he was sick of the constant protests Seattle seemed to attract. He and his fellow officers looked upon the groups smashing windows and blocking traffic with utter disdain. Coming from a military background myself, I sympathized with his view. He came up with a plan to break up one of the most radical of the protest organizations, thinking that would put him on the fast track for a promotion. He came up with the idea when I told him my neighbor, Al, had invited me to a meeting with a group he was a member of, called SNOE.

Al and I were not close friends, but we occasionally went out for drinks and burgers. I'd never spoken to him in detail about my time in the military, but sometimes I complained to him that they did not treat me well. I was thinking about the missed bronze star and time in the loony bin, but he took my complaining to mean that I hated the military and wanted to get back at them and the country in general. He idolized the soldiers who came home from Vietnam and joined the protest movements in the 70s, and just assumed most soldiers who had fought in a war came home angry at their country.

I turned down Al's offer to attend a SNOE meeting with him, but when I told Kevin about it, he told me I should go. SNOE was paranoid about who they let into their organization and trusted, but if Al vouched for me, I could get in. I was very skeptical about becoming Kevin's secret agent, but he begged me and used the brother-in-arms card to convince me to just go to one meeting. He promised me that I would not have to do anything dangerous. He just wanted me to report on what I saw and heard.

I did not want Al to think I was too eager to join his little group, so I didn't come right out and ask him if the offer to go to a meeting with him was still on the table. About a week after telling Kevin I would go undercover for him, Al asked me again if I would attend a SNOE meeting with him. This time I said yes.

One hour before the meeting started, Al came over to my apartment to go over the game plan. First, I would have to pick an alias, since nobody in SNOE used their real names. I reminded Al that we knew each other's real names. He assured me that he would take that information to the grave if I did the same for him. Al's alias was Demon, which was strange because I'd always thought of him as a pretty nice guy. I picked Sauce as my alias.

"Why Sauce?" Demon asked.

"Why not?" I replied. Sauce was a really stupid alias, but it was a passive-aggressive way for me to show my contempt for SNOE and this whole situation I'd gotten myself into.

"Okay, Sauce, it's your name, so you get to pick it," Demon said with some sarcasm.

"It's no worse than Demon," I protested.

"Demon is cool, Sauce is weird. We need to go now, SAUCE."

I didn't want to fight with Demon Al, but I didn't concede that Sauce was a worse thing to call yourself than Demon either. It was a half-hour walk to the meeting, and we had forty-five minutes before it started at eight. Demon warned me that the meetings ran long, so we stopped to fuel up our bodies on the way. I had a large plate of teriyaki and Demon had a bright red plate of extra spicy teriyaki, which was fitting given his evil alter ego.

We arrived at the meeting site on the outskirts of Chinatown in a grungy section of the city with five minutes to spare. Demon wasted no time introducing me to the leader of the group, Dagger, and his right-hand man, Deuce.

"Hey, Dagger, this is the guy I told you about. His name is Sauce." Demon said the last part with a little embarrassment.

Dagger didn't bat an eye, however, and just said, "It's good to meet you, Sauce. We can use people like you with combat experience to toughen up our ranks. We're going to turn this city and country upside down. Justice is coming, just you wait and see!" Dagger and Deuce then shook my hand and were off. Demon and I found a couple of empty chairs in the back of an overcrowded room. Around twenty-five people were attending the meeting, which Demon said was about average. If we were planning something big, then sometimes double the number of people would show up. I couldn't figure out where they would fit.

Dagger started the meeting by declaring that he had a very exciting agenda for the evening. He then went right into the cheerleading part of the session, meant to boost morale and let us know that our efforts were making a real difference in the community. A city councilman pushed through a proposal to raise corporate taxes in the city to pay for a program to distribute cash payments to poor and homeless people. This was a twofer, where it would hurt the greedy corporations and redistribute that money to the poor. In reality, the proposal was unlikely to pass or survive the inevitable Mayor's veto, if it did. It didn't matter, Dagger knew his audience and wasn't worried about the details.

Dagger didn't have a fixed agenda, other than spending the first fifteen minutes going over the group's supposed accomplishments. Demon was correct about the meeting running long. The evening devolved into endless discussions on what stances the group should take on various government policy decisions. There were some discussions on how they would apply more aggressive pressure on the city to get their message across, which boiled down to when and where they would block traffic and piss off commuters. The problem was that everybody in the room had an equal opportunity to voice their opinions, and most of the twenty-five people in the room had something to say. There were no time limits, so you could stand up and speak as long and as often as you wanted. Given the pomposity of the members of the group, nobody had the self-awareness to abridge the bullshit spewing from their mouths. It was admirable that these people spent their free time trying to make the world a better place, but I knew that nothing anybody in this room did would change anything.

# STING

It had been four months and countless meetings and protests since I started working undercover for Kevin. I told him I didn't want to narc for him anymore, but he kept convincing me that he was close to having what he needed to shut SNOE down, or at least hurt them. I didn't want out because I feared for my safety; I wanted out because attending the SNOE meetings was becoming unbearable. I couldn't stand another minute of listening to them spend hours discussing the minutiae of government policy and their plans for changing it. They even spent hours debating how they would go about staging protests, even though running into the middle of a street went about the same way every time they did it. Every discussion could just end with, we'll just do it like last week but on this road instead.

Kevin had a new plan, however. I told him that people smoked pot at the meeting, and I even spotted some of the group members doing harder drugs, like mushrooms and coke. I suspected Deuce did coke and supplied other group members with drugs. Kevin didn't think just raiding the meeting to arrest people doing illegal drugs was enough. He wanted to get Deuce on a charge that would result in a long jail sentence. If one of SNOE's leaders was charged with trafficking drugs, he thought that would be it for the whole organization.

The plan was for me to get closer to Deuce and learn more about who his dealers were, with the ultimate goal of catching him in the act of making a buy. Kevin would then arrest him on charges of buying drugs with the intent to distribute. Deuce was close to Demon, who was close to me. Because of this, we already chatted regularly before and after meetings and sometimes went out afterward for beers.

After a few drinks, I would try to subtly bring up the drug use at the meetings to see if that led to him giving me any information I could use. I thought I had blown the whole thing when he directly asked me why I was so interested in how he got his pot when I didn't even smoke it. I quickly recovered by lying that I did like to smoke pot, just not during the week. Surprisingly, he just let it go and didn't question me about my curiosity anymore. Al warned me that I should shut up about the drug use.

The close call with Deuce and the warning from Al was almost enough for me to tell Kevin I was finished being his narc. I decided to give it one more week, just to see if there was any fallout from our last outing at the bar. At the next SNOE meeting, I sat with Demon as usual, but this time Deuce also sat with us. He usually sat up front but sometimes hung out with us at the back, so I didn't think too much about it. I sat there pretending to mind my own business, while Deuce and Demon talked. Demon asked Deuce if he wanted to go out for drinks that night, but Deuce said he couldn't because he had to pick up a new supply of weed by the train tracks in Sodo.

Around thirty minutes into the meeting, I got up from my seat to go to the bathroom. I went in and checked around to see that no one was using any of the stalls, and then called Kevin to tell him what I had heard. Excitedly, he told me he would take it from there. When I sat back down in the meeting room, Deuce gave me a quick look and a smile. I should have taken that as a warning. In my haste to get back, I didn't pee, but I really did have to go to the bathroom. When I got back up to go, Demon asked where I was going, and I just held my stomach and said I must have eaten something. This time I just left the building and walked to Sodo.

I had no idea where, by the tracks in Sodo Deuce was planning to pick up his new supply of weed or what Kevin was planning. But something compelled me to be there and see this through, even though I knew at some level that I could blow the whole thing or get hurt in the crossfire. On one of the tracks was a lone freight car. I crawled under it, hid behind the wheels, and waited and waited and waited. Five hours later, I was getting very cold and stiff and considered cutting my losses and heading home. I should have realized I would be out there for hours. SNOE meetings were endless, and I'd left only forty-five minutes in.

Then, right as I was about to call it a night, I saw Deuce and somebody else I recognized from the group walking towards me. I briefly worried that they were coming for me as they circled around to the back of the freight car I was hiding under, stopped, and waited. I was hoping they were just using the train as cover like I was, since it was the only thing to hide behind in the area. After a few minutes, I started to relax, since it seemed that they weren't there to find me.

Ten minutes later, I saw one other guy in a dark jacket holding a duffle bag also walking towards the freight car. I assumed this was it and the drug deal was about to go down. The one thing I didn't see was Kevin or any other police officers. If the deal went down and Deuce wasn't arrested, this entire endeavor would have been a waste of time. As the guy in the dark jacket got closer, I started to get angry at Kevin for putting me through this for the last few months for no reason. Right now, I felt I could only continue to hide and hope they didn't spot me.

"Hey, Deuce, hey, Joey, how's it hanging?" the man in the dark jacket said as he made his way behind the car to greet his customers. They were standing on the other side of the freight car wheel, only a few feet from my location.

"It's going great, George. You got my key?" Deuce replied.

"That's why I'm here, Deuce. Let's do this. I promised the wife I'd be home for a late dinner tonight," George said.

That's when I heard, "Put your hands up and don't move!" from a loudspeaker. I then saw a lot of flashing lights coming in from all sides and officers yelling for Deuce, Joey, and George to get down on the ground. I had no idea where the cops had been hiding, and I was surprised that I hadn't seen them setting up at any time during the night while I was hiding. I then looked through the space between the wheels to see Deuce lying flat on the ground, staring at me with a big smile on his face.

After a few minutes of voices talking and rumblings from the officers, I heard one of them say, "Kevin, there is nothing here."

"What's in the duffle bag?" Kevin said.

"A key," replied the other officer.

"A key of what?" Kevin questioned.

"That's what I'm trying to tell you, it is just literally a big key," the other officer answered.

Kevin cursed angrily. He screamed at the trio, asking where the drugs were. They just answered that they didn't know what he was talking about. Finally, Kevin told the other officers to let them go. Some of the cops started laughing and ribbing Kevin. They told him his narc had really fucked him, which would be me. I just lay there knowing that I had been played by Deuce. When I started poking him about where he got his weed from, he must have suspected something and arranged this whole thing to set me up and make the cops look like fools.

I wasn't worried about Kevin or any other cop right now. Deuce now knew I was a police informer, so I was worried about my life. When the cops cleared out, I walked home, hoping whatever was going to happen to me wouldn't happen tonight. The next morning, I called Kevin to ask what had happened.

"The fucker set us up. We swarmed in as soon we saw them making the deal, but none of them had any drugs or money on them. My career is over," Kevin complained.

"Fuck your career, my life might be over. They know I'm the informant now. I need police protection!" I demanded.

"I'll be lucky to still have a job by the end of the day. I'll ask, but they're not going to listen to me anymore," Kevin said dejectedly.

I was on my own. I hoped that making me and the police look stupid would be enough for Deuce, but I doubted it. I got dressed and went to work as usual but kept my head on a swivel. My stress levels were through the roof. Later that day, when I got home and saw Al, I prepared myself for the inevitable angry confrontation, but he just smiled at me and asked me if my stomach felt better. After a short pause to compose myself and hide my relief, I told him I felt a little better, but needed to stay in tonight. He said he understood, and we walked up to our floor together and entered our separate apartments.

I wasn't sure what Al not knowing meant in the long run, but at least my betrayal of the socialist cause was not common knowledge yet. A couple of weeks later, there was still no blowback from the failed sting operation. Kevin had been demoted to traffic cop, but I was still alive, and Al still didn't know what had happened. I did tell Al I was quitting SNOE and wouldn't be attending any more meetings or protests. He tried to encourage me to stick with it, but I just told him it didn't feel right for me anymore, without giving him any details about why that was. That seemed to also end our friendship since he stopped talking to me altogether after that.

# BURIED ALIVE

It was late on a Tuesday night, and I was walking home from work. Our computer network at work had caught a virus, so it was all hands-on deck. At midnight, I finally had to get home to get some sleep but promised them I would be back early the next morning to continue repairing the system. Besides, there were a couple of younger workers who could hold the fort until I got back in the morning.

As I walked down the street, I was very tired and consumed with thoughts about how I was going to fix the system and make sure it was more resistant to virus attacks in the future. I took a shortcut through a wide alleyway that I usually avoided. As I walked through the dark alley, I suddenly felt a sharp pain in the back of my head.

I woke up confused, not remembering what had happened. I had a horrible headache that emanated from the back of my head. I tried to rub the source of pain with my hand, but then quickly realized that I couldn't move them. They were tied behind my back. I also then noticed I was in a dark confined space getting bumped around. There was a radio playing heavy metal music in the background. I was in the trunk of a moving car. I also noticed the front of my pants was wet, which led to a moment of self-hate and embarrassment.

I had no idea how long I had been in the trunk, but the drive seemed to last a very long time after I woke up. I needed to do something, so I started wiggling my hands back and forth to loosen the rope binding my wrists together. My hands broke free in less than a minute. I then lay there waiting for what would come next; like I had a choice.

After a little while, the road got much bumpier. I bounced around the trunk like a beach ball. I just held my arms over my head to avoid a second concussion. Then the car came to an abrupt stop, which threw me into the back of the trunk. The music stopped and I heard a car door open and then slam shut. I heard nothing for a few more minutes and wondered if I was being abandoned. What I heard next put a little shiver down my spine. In the distance, I heard digging. The digging went on for what could have been almost an hour before it stopped.

A while later I heard footsteps coming towards the back of the car and the trunk popped open. I had kept my hands partially hidden to hide the fact that I was free from the restraints, but after the trunk opened, I saw a head and torso lean in towards me and made my move.

I grabbed the neck in a bear hug and squeezed with all I had. I managed to kick myself out of the trunk and landed on my adversary's back with my arms still wrapped around his neck, squeezing. He tried to wiggle free and kick me, but I was much stronger, and he was quickly losing oxygen. When I felt him go limp, I let go and caught a few breaths, and then turned him over. It was Deuce.

After checking that he was still alive, I found the rope and tied his wrists together with a proper knot. I also found some tape when I searched his car and secured his wrists again with the tape, as well as his ankles and mouth. The idiot would have had me if he'd just taped my wrists together. In my search of the car and his pockets, I found his wallet and car papers. His real name was Brad. Looking down on him, I realized now that he was just a skinny guy with very little muscle. I couldn't believe I had been scared of him.

The other thing I found around thirty feet from where the car was parked was a very large hole in the ground, so it was no wonder I'd heard him digging for almost an hour. I was actually a little impressed he'd managed it in that amount of time. He was awake now, so it was time to talk.

"What's up, Brad? I see you've been busy. Were you planning on burying me alive?" I asked.

All I heard in response was "Mmmmm, Mmmmm," and a fearful look. I leaned over to remove the tape from his mouth.

"No, man, no, I was just going to scare you and take you back home. I swear. You can't say you didn't deserve it after trying to get me arrested, can you?"

"Actually, I can, Brad, say I didn't deserve to be buried alive," I ominously replied.

"No, no, no, I promise, I was just going to let you go!" He was really scared now. He wet his pants, which made me feel a little better about my accident. Of course, I wet my pants while unconscious.

"Where are we?" I asked.

"We're just off in some back road by Lake Cavanaugh. I swear I wasn't going to hurt you!"

I covered his mouth back up. I was sick of his lies. I had no idea where Lake Cavanaugh was but assumed I could find my way out. I really wish he'd died in the fight since that would have been self-defense. If I kill him now, it would be murder. At least in the eyes of the law, if I was caught. I spent a long time playing the pros and cons of dumping him in his own hole. I'm sure I'd killed better people than him in Iraq. Ultimately, I decided to just throw him in the trunk and drive home, hoping he'd learned his lesson and realized he wasn't a badass.

Finding my way back along the road he drove in and ultimately back to I-5 wasn't too hard. My biggest worry was getting stopped by the police and them discovering that I was driving someone else's car with the owner tied up in the trunk. Getting thrown in jail for assault and kidnapping would be the perfect way to cap off this awful night and the last few months. I also had to worry about Brad reporting me to the police but didn't think he would. I hoped that he would just want this whole thing behind him, like I did. I didn't want to regret not burying him.

When I got back home, I found an abandoned lot around a mile from my apartment and dumped the car with the trunk open, but I left Brad tied up. I assumed somebody would come by and find him in the morning. I gave him a warning that I was going to tell my cop friend and my other army buddies everything about what happened that night, so if I disappeared or turned up dead, he would be the top suspect. It was 4:30 AM when I got home and I just fell into bed, exhausted.

It had been a few weeks since the attempted murder, and no police had shown up at my door to arrest me. I didn't read in the newspaper or hear from Al that Deuce/Brad had been found dead. I started to relax a little. I think the warning I gave him probably worked. I really did tell Kevin the whole story. He asked me if I wanted to press charges, but when I said no, he was relieved. He wanted all this behind him too. I gave him Brad's full name and address. Kevin promised he would stop by his place and warn him off. We met for breakfast at a local café a couple of months after the incident. Kevin had some news for me.

"I'm going back to Georgia," Kevin said.

"You're quitting the police force?"

"Yep, after making a fool of myself, I've been told that my career is dead. If I stay in Seattle, I'll just be directing traffic for the rest of my life. It's a miracle those assholes didn't press charges or go to the press screaming about police brutality," Kevin said.

"I'm sure that was an option on the table, but they went with burying me alive instead," I stated.

"I reckon you're probably right," Kevin replied flatly with a little smile on his face. "Don't worry about me. For the last couple of years, my high school buddy, who's a deputy in my hometown, has been trying to get me to leave Seattle and join the police force down there. I've accepted, so now I'm moving back home to be a cop there."

"You hate your hometown!"

"Supposedly, it's changed a lot. Most of the hard asses have passed and a lot of newcomers have moved in. It's now considered a suburb of Atlanta, even though it's an hour's drive away."

"They don't care about what happened here?" I asked.

"It probably helps me. People in Georgia think people from Seattle are just a bunch of pussy freaks."

We finished our breakfast. I had the Denver omelet and hash browns, which were delicious. After a quick bro-hug, we went off in our separate directions. I never saw or heard from Kevin again, but assumed he met a nice Southern girl and lived happily ever after.

# START UP

The day started like every Tuesday morning, with a three-mile run, a quick shower, some eggs, and tea, and then off to work. I was sitting at my desk, deep into writing another script to automate moving data from one data store to another, which was part of my typical day working IT, when I got the call from Leo. I could tell right away that Leo was very excited about something. He normally gets right to the subject at hand, without drawing things out with questions and filler words, but after picking up the phone, his first words were, "What are you doing? You're not going to believe this. Oh boy..."

"Is everything all right?" I expressed with concern.

"This is it! We've got our in," he said excitedly.

"What are you talking about, Leo? I'm busy here."

"Sorry, sorry, you know how we've been dreaming about getting in with a startup? Well, I just met two guys building a startup and they need two developers. They want us to join them."

Leo and I had both made decent livings, but we always talked about what it would be like to be one of those people who got in early on a new startup and struck it rich. Being in the tech industry, all you hear about is people getting super rich by founding a company that gets bought out or cashing in those stock options. We were several years into the new century and working our salaried jobs wasn't cutting it anymore, but we didn't know how to (or maybe we were just too risk-averse or lazy) go about changing our situations.

Over the next few minutes, Leo gave me all the details. He had been discreetly interviewing for new positions at a job fair a couple of weeks ago and met two guys named Jan and Sanjay. Jan and Sanjay had started a company named BA Services; BA stood for Business Augmentation. The three of them came up with a plan to sell a service that "enhanced and highlighted" positive customer reviews to boost a business's profile and attract more customers. Jan and Sanjay were the company founders and claimed to already have a million dollars in funding.

They offered Leo a three percent share of the company to lead the engineering department. He had the budget to hire one additional developer and he could offer that hire a one percent share of the company, which was why Leo had called me. He made the case that even if the company at worst was sold down the road for $100,000,000, that would still leave me with $1,000,000 with my one percent share. At best, it would be worth a lot more or the company would go public and possibly be worth billions someday. The downside was that I would only be paid $1500 a month before taxes and there were no benefits, like health insurance, included. To be fair, that was all Leo was getting paid too. Jan and Sanjay told Leo that they were living together in a group house so that every cent they raised for the startup could be re-invested in the company. We would all be in this together.

I was somewhat prepared for this. When Leo and I daydreamed about making it big with a startup, we thought of people like Bezos or Jobs who started companies in their garages without any idea if they would succeed or fail. If BA Services failed, I could always go back to working in IT, so I decided it was time to take a risk, and this seemed like too good an opportunity to pass on. Especially, since I'd be working with Leo, my old friend from the Bronx, and I just had to slip into the plan they had already laid out.

Two weeks later, I'd quit my job and started my first day at BA Services. All four of us met in a small space we rented in the Pioneer Square neighborhood of Seattle. It was a dump, but it had working electricity and enough room for around ten people to set up their desks and work. That was enough, since it was only Leo and I coming in daily for the time being. Jan had prepared a PowerPoint presentation to mark our first day in the office. The first few slides talked about how BA Services would disrupt the industry. I asked Jan what industry we were disrupting and how, which seemed to annoy him. He answered that businesses that subscribed to our service would be the winners in the new internet age. Getting more customers was all about positive social media presence and online visibility. We provided that.

The presentation concluded with how our sacrifices today would lead to a better world tomorrow. According to our founders, we weren't only disrupting the entire tech industry, but also making the world a better place by connecting people and businesses, hence building up stronger communities. It looked great on a slide deck. In this new world, Leo and I would build the service for little pay now, but riches later, and the founders would take their presentation around Silicon Valley to drum up more capital and sign on future subscribers. It seemed a little half-baked to me, but I'd never been part of a startup before, so I assumed that it always started like this. All the internet companies raking in millions had probably started with a presentation about how they were going to change the world.

After the presentation, we had a brainstorming session and came up with the name, RevGen, for our service, which was short for review generator. World domination was going to start with building a service that posted positive reviews on the popular business review website, Yauzzers. A business would pay us a monthly fee to generate an agreed-upon number of positive reviews. I suppose we were disrupting the competitors of said businesses, as they would have lower review ratings than those who signed up for our service.

Before we could disrupt the industry and change the world, we had to actually build the product, or so I thought. To secure more funding and start selling RevGen, Jan and Sanjay needed a demo to go along with their pitch. Working twenty-hour days for the next two weeks, Leo and I put together a video of us using the product. The video showed our service automatically creating Yauzzers user accounts and posting good reviews from those accounts. The reviews all seemed like they were written by real human beings and not generated by a computer. Nobody reading them could tell they were fake. Of course, the reviews in our demo *were* written by real humans, but that fact was left out of the presentation.

The demo was useful to Leo and me since it gave us a goal to work towards. We would ship RevGen in six months, with limited availability. Users who signed up in advance with a deposit would be first in line to use our service, and we would slowly add new users as we ramped up our computing resources. This meant the company could start generating revenue immediately, which would help fund hiring more developers and the marketing campaign. The goal was to start paying ourselves more, after RevGen was officially released and the real money started rolling in.

It only took around a week for Leo and me to come up with the overall design. RevGen would read reviews for a particular business and then duplicate reviews of the star rating we wanted to amplify. This was the easy part, and we had that up and running after only two weeks of development effort. To make it more useful, we had to write a program to modify those duplicated reviews, so we weren't just posting identical reviews that could easily be identified as fake. We also had to build a service that created Yauzzers accounts for posting fake reviews. Leo and I could work on the former problem, but to generate fake Yauzzers accounts, we had to hire a hacker experienced in building botnets.

Fortunately, Jan had a contact who was experienced in hacking into corporate networks and stealing information to sell or cause mischief. The hacker called himself Kingpin; we didn't know his real name. He decided to give himself a new alias, Magnum, to use at BA

Services. Unfortunately, he insisted on getting paid real money, unlike the rest of us. I was told he'd signed up for a six-month contract for $100,000 to build the service and deploy it. He would also be paid more money in the future to run the service based on our company's revenue. The money was paid in advance to an offshore bank account that Magnum had set up. He worked remotely, so we only communicated with him over e-mail.

In addition to having access to Magnum's botnet that could create Yauzzers user accounts and post our fake reviews, he would help Leo and I build the program that duplicated reviews with modifications to make them unique. Over the course of the next couple of months, we made progress on our review modifier. Its main function was to replace adjectives and common phrasing we saw used in many reviews. For example, "I loved the enchiladas" might be modified to "I really liked the enchiladas" or "The service was excellent" to "The server did an excellent job." Most of our time was spent reading reviews and building replacement phrases, for phrases we would see in those reviews. In addition, we would take reviews from one restaurant or business of the same type and re-post them with the fake account to the business we were trying to prop up or bring down. Sanjay insisted that we also offer businesses an option to bring down their competitors' ratings; in addition to increasing their own ratings.

Three months after we first came up with our idea, we were ready to deploy our review modifier to RevGen. The problem was that Magnum still hadn't delivered the botnet for creating fake Yauzzers accounts. In fact, we barely heard from Magnum at all anymore. For the first couple of months, we would share our review modifier ideas with him, looking for feedback. He would send us short replies, like "That's cool" or "You guys are really hitting it out of the park" and other useless motivational feedback.

Jan and Sanjay were not much help in getting us information as to when Magnum would deliver his botnet. After weeks of Leo and I requesting to meet with them, we all finally sat down together five months into the project to review our progress. Sanjay led the meeting off, asking us why we hadn't delivered the service yet. Leo and I just looked at each other and I started by giving him our progress with the review modifier. Jan interrupted me just as I started getting into the details, asking when we could turn the new service on and start generating reviews. Sanjay then came in letting me know that they had already sold over two million dollars' worth of subscriptions to our service and those initial customers expected us to go live in just four weeks from now.

I knew they were selling deposits to customers who wanted to be first in line to use RevGen, but I never expected them to sell two million dollars' worth of subscriptions and promise we would go live by a set date. I asked Sanjay how he had sold so many subscriptions. This was a point of pride for Jan and Sanjay, so they eagerly gave us the details. They'd spent weeks dead-calling and showing up at the front doors of small businesses around the San Fransisco and Silicon Valley area looking to pre-sell RevGen. After over a month of failure, they finally got one newly opened restaurant to sign a heavily discounted contract to use our service for six months. They agreed to pay for the first month as a deposit and then pay the rest month to month after we started posting good reviews.

Based on that first sale, they went to other restaurants and started playing them against each other. "Look at all the good reviews your competitors are getting, so you better get in on this too," sort of sales pitch. With some restaurants, they even went a step further and warned them that without us protecting them, a competitor could use our service to post negative reviews of their restaurant and bring them down. These were real mob tactics, but Jan and Sanjay didn't seem to have any qualms about selling RevGen this way. In addition to restaurants, they targeted Yoga studios and lawn care businesses.

# GOING LIVE

Leo and I spent the rest of the night in the office trying to figure out what to do about the mess the founders had created. We could just walk away, but then we would get nothing for our hard work except the meager pay we had already received. At 4:00 AM, it dawned on me (no pun intended) what needed to be done. We'd already counted out Magnum delivering his botnet in the next couple of days, and even if he did, we didn't think we could put the whole service together in under a month. We didn't even have servers to run the service. We had nothing except for a heuristics-based review generator that ran on our PCs.

My plan was to simply hire people on the cheap to write reviews, sort of like how telemarketing worked. We would hire people who didn't mind working at a mind-numbing job for minimum wage. Fortunately, there were people who needed work badly enough to take the job. On the plus side, you could work as many or as few hours as you wanted, and we provided free grocery store brand soda, ramen, and bagels and cream cheese at the office.

The next day we took our proposal to Jan and Sanjay, and they quickly agreed to our plan. The budget was $1500.00 a week, which meant we could hire five to six people. We posted our job listing in the Seattle Times and a couple of job posting websites. The listing was short and to the point.

*"Get in on the ground floor of a high-flying tech startup. BA Services was founded on the principles of serving our customers while making the world a better place. As a founding member of our team, your job is to work with businesses to improve their sales and online presence using BA Services' cutting-edge technology. Benefits at signing include ten stock options and the chance to earn bonuses and additional stock options, free food, and drinks."*

It was Jan's idea to add the ten stock options. Like us, other people might be lured in by the chance to get rich. Young people also liked free food, so we thought ramen would balance out the low pay. He sent us over a contract for new hires to sign that spelled out their terms of employment and promised them ten stock options in BA Services at $5.00 a share. The day after we posted the job listing, we fielded over a hundred calls inquiring about the job. We brought in around thirty candidates for interviews and hired six new college graduates at $7.01 an hour. We told them all to come in for their orientation the following Monday at 9:00 AM sharp, which gave Leo and I five days to set up an office and figure out what they would do.

We lucked out setting up the office. Another company in the area was closing their offices and was unloading their office equipment, including desks, chairs, and computers. The PCs were a couple of generations out of date, but that didn't matter for what our staff would be doing. In addition, we bought a used refrigerator to store the free food we'd promised. We also took the heuristics we built into RevGen for duplicating reviews and wrote them out in a step-by-step guide for the new hires to follow.

Monday morning, all six hires showed up and after Sanjay went over the NDA and they had all signed it, he left, and we got down to business. Leo and I spent the rest of the day showing them exactly what we wanted them to do and how. They all got to practice setting up a Yauzzers account and writing new reviews based on our guides. Before posting a review, Leo or I always had to approve it first. The next day, our new human-powered RevGen replacement was up and running. We had twenty-three clients that first week, all signed up to receive ten good reviews a day. In addition, three of the customers signed up for us to post bad reviews to their competitors. It meant our six employees only had to generate 290 reviews a day in total. They only had to average writing one review every 10 minutes, so for those first few weeks, we all had a lot of free time on our hands to goof around.

One of the team members, named Jamal, brought in a ping pong table and we had daily tournaments. We also bought beer and played drinking games. For example, the last person to finish their daily quota of reviews had to chug a beer. We also required the person who wrote the nastiest negative review to chug a beer, judged by Leo and me. By the third week, our office seemed more like a frat house than a place of business. All our shenanigans distracted us from the unethical work we were doing. We were all starting to feel a little dirty, especially when it came to posting negative reviews.

Jan and Sanjay were busy signing up new customers too. By week four, our customer base had jumped from twenty-three to forty. The next week we had fifty-four customers, and the week after that we had seventy-three. Business was booming, and we could no longer keep up writing reviews, even with Leo and I writing them alongside the six team members. We got approval to hire six more people to handle the additional load of reviews. Given the dirty work we were doing and the party atmosphere, we made sure to hire people we felt were morally compromised. The two women from the original six both quit, so we decided to keep it an all-male office to perpetuate the frat vibe.

Now there were fourteen of us squeezed into a space that could barely hold ten. We let Sanjay know that we would need a bigger office, but he just said maybe in the future. I knew that he had a really good deal on the lease to our current space and wasn't looking to spend any more money than he had to, even with business booming. When Leo and I brought up increasing our pay, we also got ambiguous responses, promising that they would look into it in the future. After a few months, the workload was so high that beer and donuts were no longer enough to make up for the low pay for everyone in the office. Since Leo and I managed the office, all the complaints were directed at us. Each week, one or two team members would quit, but so far, we had been able to quickly replace them.

One of our solutions to increase review writing throughput was to let quality slide. We no longer reviewed any of the reviews the staff wrote before they were posted. The result was we had one five-star review posted, that praised the ass of a waitress who worked at one of our customer's restaurants. That was matched with a one-star review of their competitor, that complained the wait staff smelled so bad that the customer threw up in their salad and was in talks with a lawyer about suing the establishment for damages. We spammed one restaurant with over five hundred fake reviews claiming food poisoning.

BA Services' clients were getting upset, which meant that they were contacting Jan and Sanjay. In turn, the founders would call Leo and me up to chew us out. For $1500 a month, we just didn't care anymore and assumed we would get fired eventually. We did have contracts guaranteeing our shared ownership in the company, so we still had delusional hopes that we would get rich off this someday.

Seven months in and countless employee turnovers, no progress on salary raises or a larger office space, things finally came tumbling down. The first clue that something was off was when we stopped getting paychecks. First thing, every Monday morning, I would have weekly paychecks for all of the staff, Leo and I included, for work we had done the previous week. I lied to the staff that the paychecks were delayed until the afternoon in order to get everybody back to work. In the meantime, Leo frantically tried to get a hold of either Jan or Sanjay to ask what was happening with our pay.

After waiting two more days and still not receiving the paychecks or getting a hold of either Jan or Sanjay, we just told everyone to go home and promised we would get back to them as soon as we resolved the issue. Of course, the staff were very angry, having now worked seven days without pay, and that anger was directed solely at Leo and me. It only placated them slightly when we told them we hadn't been paid either. In fact, I also hadn't been reimbursed for all the food and drinks I'd bought for the office in over a month.

The next week, Leo and I knew that the company was dead, and we likely weren't getting our paychecks, but we were still coming to work each day trying to reach the founders. We were both in the office when federal officers showed up to confiscate all of our equipment and take Leo and me in for questioning. Apparently, the FTC had opened a case against us based on complaints from our customers and irregularities involving Jan and Sanjay's sales tactics and management of the money they were pulling in.

When we were brought into the federal building in Seattle, Leo and I were split up. I was taken into a small room with a mirror. There was a wooden table in the center of the room with two chairs on one side and a single chair on the other. I was placed in the single chair and told an officer would be in with me in a minute. There was no clock in the room and I wasn't wearing a watch, but the wait was much longer than a minute. After sitting there for a while, I started to feel some tightness in my bladder and started to worry about when I would get to go to the bathroom. After a while, the pain started to get worse, and I really had to go. I got up and tried the door, but it was locked. I started asking the mirror if I could go to the bathroom, with the hope there was somebody on the other side, like in the movies. I sat back down in my chair and curled up a little, trying to relax myself and not pee my pants. That would definitely make me look guilty.

Finally, a woman walked in with an empty Styrofoam cup and a pot of coffee. She put the cup down on the table in front of me and then slowly started filling it as I begged her to let me go to the bathroom. She just smiled at me and nodded while continuing to slowly fill the cup. I lost it and wet my pants. She just said, "Oh my," before finishing the fill and leaving me there sitting in my own puddle of urine. At this point, I lost all of my dignity, so I just finished peeing until my bladder was empty.

Ten minutes later, a man and woman walked in with an orange jumpsuit and a pair of boxers. The man said, "Carol told me you had an accident. Unfortunately, this jumpsuit is the only dry clothes I could find."

Looking at the prison garb, I asked, "Am I under arrest?"

"Not yet," the woman answered.

"Then can I just go?"

The male responded, "Technically yes, but then we'd have to read you your rights and formally arrest you. I think it would be better for all of us to just keep this casual for now. You'll be home before you know it. Does that sound good?"

I looked at them, and against my better judgment, I agreed to stay. They smiled, thanked me, and left the room again, telling me they would be right back. As soon as they left, a man with a mop walked in to clean up my mess while I changed in the corner. I just tossed my soiled pants and underwear in his garbage bucket and put on the jumpsuit, stuffing my wallet in the jumpsuit's front pocket. There was a vent in the ceiling, but after he left and closed the door, my eyes started to sting and water from the bleach odor, so now I looked like I was crying. I was certain the two officers were on the other side of that mirror, eating nachos and laughing their heads off.

After another long indeterminate amount of time, the man and woman officers finally came back in. The man introduced himself as Agent Darry and introduced the woman as Agent McMullen. Agent McMullen started by assuring me that things like that happen from time to time and I shouldn't be embarrassed about it. It was like I was being comforted by a date about not being able to get it up. I'm sure they were just trying to break down the computer geek, but after the impotent comment, I just became enraged. I wasn't going to make it easy on them.

"Look, McMullen, I think you hurt his feelings."

McMullen just smiled. Agent Darry focused his attention back on me. He took out a notepad and started asking questions. He started simply with, "Please describe what BA Services does, in your view?"

"It is a tech startup."

"What is your business model?"

"We help our clients," I responded tersely.

"Okaaay, but how do you help your clients?"

"I'm just an employee, I don't know the big picture."

"Well, Simon, we both know that isn't true. According to your business license, you are part owner of BA Services and not just an employee," Agent McMullen interjected. She then handed me a document showing that Leo and I were the sole proprietors, each owning 50% of the company.

After a minute of silence, Agent Darry chimed in again, "You can see why you might want to be more cooperative. BA Services has been involved in a lot of troubling dealings and according to all of the company paperwork, BA Services is you and your friend Leo's.

I actually didn't see why I should cooperate at this point, so I said I wanted to consult a lawyer. Agent Darry reminded me that I wasn't under arrest yet, so I asked if I could leave. They let me go but warned me not to try to leave town. When I got outside, I was surprised it was dark. I had been there all day. I needed to get in touch with Leo but didn't know if he was home or still getting interrogated. I decided to try the office first and see if I could call him from there.

The office was a mess. All the computers were gone, along with any notepads that were sitting on the desks of the staff. It seemed like they had purposely trashed the place. The refrigerator was left open and some of the chairs were overturned on the floor. The phones still worked, but I could not get hold of Leo. I couldn't get hold of Jan or Sanjay either, which wasn't surprising. After sitting there in the dark for a while, I noticed how hungry I was, so I left, not bothering to clean anything up. I wasn't coming back.

A few minutes later, at Taco Bell, I noticed people kept looking at me. I was so stressed that it took me a while to realize that I was still wearing a bright orange jumpsuit with the word "prison" written on it. I just turned to the person next to me, opened my eyes real wide, and loudly said, "Laundry day!" I guess that I smelled like pee too, so I'm sure some of the diners thought I was homeless. I thought to myself that I could make it up to the restaurant by throwing them a few five-star reviews for free. After that thought, I couldn't stop laughing at my own lame humor, which most certainly made me come across as crazed. The person at the table next to me got up and moved to the other side of the restaurant.

I suddenly felt very tired. I couldn't think straight and stumbled home like the hobo I was morphing into. Despite all my troubles, I fell asleep as soon as my head hit the pillow.

# GOING DOWN

I woke up to hard knocking on my door. I was lying on my stomach with the sun shining brightly on the back of my head. I felt a little hungover, though I hadn't drunk anything the day before. My head cleared quickly as I noticed that my stomach was rumbling, and I had seconds to get to the bathroom. As I ran across the room, I screamed at the person banging on my door that I would be there in a second, and then managed to get on the toilet just in time. Unfortunately, I didn't manage to get my orange jumpsuit pulled down before I sat down. This was my second accident in two days. I could just imagine that McMullen was standing outside my door laughing her ass off.

The banging on the door started up again, along with "Yo Simon, it's me, Leo. We have to talk."

I screamed back, "Now's not a good time."

"What the fuck do you mean it's not a good time. We have to talk about what happened now!" Leo replied angrily.

"Okay, Okay, can you go walk around the block or something? I'll be ready in ten minutes."

"Why, just let me in! What's that smell?"

"No, ten minutes."

"What the fuck, Simon? Fine, I'm going to the café down on the corner. Just meet me there."

Thankfully, I was alone again and packed up my soiled prison garb into a garbage bag and showered. Feeling much better now that the burrito was out of my system, I walked down to the café to meet Leo, dumping my nastiness into the garbage shoot on the way out. I hoped the agents hadn't secretly bugged my apartment with cameras, since I wanted to keep this second accident to myself.

When I got to the café, I saw that Leo was sitting in a booth in the back with a cup of coffee. I decided to start things off lightly, so I led with "Where's my coffee?"

"You don't drink coffee?" he answered, confused.

Now that the small talk was out of the way, I sat down and we recapped what had happened at the Federal building the night before. I left out the part about peeing myself but did mention the papers that showed Leo and me as BA Services' owners. Leo's experience was similar to mine, though he didn't mention peeing himself either. We both realized that Jan and Sanjay were running a scam and had made us the fall guys. We had to prove that we didn't own BA Services and were also victims of the scam. The first step was to hire a lawyer. Luckily, Leo found a lawyer who specialized in defending businesses accused of fraud through a friend of his. We had our first meeting with him that afternoon. Leo forebodingly said I should check my bank account before the meeting; whatever the outcome, this was going to be expensive.

Our lawyer's office was on one of the top floors of a downtown skyscraper. The lobby screamed old money, with dark red carpeting and dark paneling on all other surfaces. I felt like I'd stepped back into the early twentieth century. I hoped his expensive tastes in decorating would translate to skill in the courtroom. A grandmotherly, conservatively dressed secretary in bright white sneakers, named Ms. Ecker, came in and led us to Mr. Johnson's office, which was decorated in the same style as the lobby. Mr. Johnson was also quite old, which probably explained the classic look of his offices. Ms. Ecker offered us both coffee, which Leo accepted. I asked if I could have a cup of tea, to which she responded with a slight nod, "but of course."

We quickly recapped our adventures of the previous day. When we got to the question of ownership, it got a little awkward. While Mr. Johnson accepted that Leo and I were not the sole owners of BA Services, we did admit that Leo may have owned three percent of the company, and I owned one percent. Given the forged documents, it wasn't clear if there was any hard evidence showing what our initial agreement was with Jan and Sanjay. We decided that we would continue to insist that Jan and Sanjay were the real owners of the company and only reveal our employment agreement if asked directly. Given the FTC had probably been investigating BA Services for some time, we all assumed they knew it was Jan and Sanjay in Silicon Valley drumming up capital and signing up customers. Leo and I were just left holding the bag.

Three days later, I was back in the interrogation room, but this time with Leo and Mr. Johnson by my side. Agents Darry and McMullen were already waiting for us when we were brought to the room. With our lawyer present, they cut the enhanced interrogation tactics out. McMullen looked me in the eye and breezily said, "You clean up nice," and gave me a little wink. Leo and Mr. Johnson looked at me a little confused, but I just shrugged my shoulders like I didn't know what she was talking about. Mr. Johnson took charge and asked the agents to stop harassing his clients. With the fun at my expense over, we got down to the interview.

It started with Agent Darry announcing that he was turning on a recording device. He then stated the purpose of the meeting and the people present in the room. With that out of the way, he asked me what my role as owner of BA Services was. I started to answer, but Mr. Johnson cut me off and answered, "My clients' ownership of BA Services has not been established."

"According to BA Services' business license, Mr. Diaz and Mr. Zane are the legal owners," Agent Darry replied.

"That is an obvious forgery," Mr. Johnson continued.

"We confirmed that the signatures are a match for Mr. Diaz and Mr. Zane."

"I do not doubt that, but you know as well as I that a signature match is meaningless in this case. Those signatures were simply lifted from some other document and transferred to the business license."

More aggressively, Agent Darry replied, "No, that is not clear. The way I see it, Mr. Diaz and Mr. Zane are clearly the owners of BA Services."

Mr. Johnson took a long pause and then calmly said, "Let's please stop the charade, we all know that Jan and Sanjay are who you are really after and the true founders of BA Services. Records show that they were recruiting at job fairs in the Seattle area before my clients joined the company. You also know that they were the ones in Silicon Valley securing venture capital and selling the product in question to customers."

Now it was McMullen's turn to chime in. "If what you say is true, can you tell us where these alternative owners are right now? Can you give us their full names?"

"My clients do not know the location of Jan and Sanjay." Mr. Johnson then consulted with us for a few seconds and then went on, "Unfortunately, they do not know Jan and Sanjay's last names."

"You are telling us that after working with what you claim are the real owners for over a half a year, you don't even know their names?" McMullen replied with exasperation.

"The owners only ever identified themselves by their first names. The office environment was casual."

"Yes, casual is a good word. While earning millions of dollars from your investors and customers, you were casually destroying businesses and peoples' livelihoods by running a fake review mill," Darry stated.

This got to the heart of the matter. Even though Jan and Sanjay were the real founders, we went along with it, even though we both knew what we were doing was wrong and hurting people.

Mr. Johnson then politely asked, "Agent Darry and Agent McMullen, my clients have done nothing illegal. We are here only as a courtesy to help you with your investigation. If you are not charging my clients and have no further questions, we should end this meeting now."

Exasperated, Agent Darry shut off the recorder. He looked at Leo and me and told us that we should be ashamed of ourselves. They promised to be back in contact with us shortly. Mr. Johnson insisted that they contact his office directly. After we left the Federal building, we huddled for a few minutes to go over what we'd learned.

Mr. Johnson started with, "They don't have any concrete evidence against you that would constitute a crime – yet. They were just fishing for information and hoping you would incriminate yourselves or tell them where Jan and Sanjay were. Since they are Indian nationals, I suspect they are no longer in the country and our agent friends know it. That is why they are after you two."

"Okay, but what do we do now?" Leo asked.

"We just wait. If they want more information from you on what occurred at BA Services, they'll need to offer you some kind of deal, so you avoid incriminating yourselves."

"We don't know that much about what Jan and Sanjay were doing in Silicon Valley. We just ran the office," I said.

"You did more than that, and you know more about what they were doing than you're letting on. Hopefully, you'll get some type of immunity deal so you can tell the full story to Agents Darry and McMullen," Mr. Johnson replied. He then assured us that he would get back to us after he was contacted again by the agents, and we went our separate ways.

After both Agent Darry and my lawyer had admonished me and I realized that I wasn't really innocent in this whole affair, I was feeling pretty down. Leo and I walked together for a couple of blocks and then went our separate ways. We both wanted to be alone. I decided to eat away my sorrows. I walked about a mile to an Italian restaurant I'd heard was very good and ordered the veal Parmesan. I wasn't going to waste my sorrows on bad food and, as predicted, the food was amazing. I wasn't a big drinker, but I also polished off a whole bottle of wine and finished the night with a delicious tiramisu.

I was overstuffed and my head was spinning from the wine, so I barely remembered my walk home when I got up the next day. I was just happy I was in one piece and seemed to still have my wallet on me. I also had the receipt which showed my restaurant bill was $153. I'd also left a $50 tip. This was a lot more money than I could afford to spend, especially given my upcoming lawyer bills. I needed to get a hold of myself.

To even out my food bill, I spent the next couple of days holed up in my apartment eating bagels and cream cheese and ramen. It was food I had bought for the now-defunct office. I expected Agents Darry and McMullen to knock on my door at any time with an arrest warrant, so I just wanted to spend as much time as possible sitting in my apartment and pretending that everything was normal. That also meant not talking to Leo, since inevitably the subject would move toward what was happening with the investigation.

Three days after the last interview at the Federal building, Ms. Ecker called me at 9:00 AM and asked me to be at Mr. Johnson's office at 2:00 PM sharp. I used the outing as an opportunity to shave and clean myself up. I was back in the Victorian-styled waiting room forty-five minutes before the scheduled meeting. This allowed me time to read two full issues of People Magazine before Leo finally arrived a full minute before two.

We sat down in Mr. Johnson's office. Ms. Ecker already had our coffee and tea orders ready for us; she was very efficient. Besides the refreshments, Mr. Johnson skipped over the niceties and got right down to business. "I've been negotiating with our friends at the FTC for the better part of the last two days, and I think I have a settlement that both of you should seriously consider."

Mr. Johnson then shuffled some papers around and found the one he was looking for. He then continued, "You can read the full agreement before signing it, but it is available to both or either of you, though I strongly advise against one of you rejecting it if the other signs it. In a nutshell, the agreement gets you immunity from further prosecution if you plead guilty to committing internet fraud as a misdemeanor."

Leo interjected, "Wait, why do we need to plead guilty if they don't have anything on us?"

Annoyed, Mr. Johnson continued, "Let me finish. Along with the charges, you will each get five years of probation where you'll no longer be allowed to post reviews of a service or product on any media platform or use social media. In addition, you'll each pay a $10,000 fine. Of course, while you won't be open to any new federal charges, there is still the possibility that one of the businesses you hurt could sue you. I don't think that is

190

likely, but you never know." Leo started to talk again, but Mr. Johnson held up his hand and continued, "In return for immunity, you'll also be required to reveal everything you know about BA Services, Jan, and Sanjay to Agents Darry and McMullen. The deal is off if you do not fully cooperate. As the registered owners of BA Services, you'll give them permission to access all of the company records. That's all."

We both looked at Leo, so he could finally get his thoughts in. "When we last met with the Agents, we agreed they had no real evidence that we did anything wrong. Why should we plead guilty?"

"First off, we didn't agree that you did nothing wrong. At the time, it seemed like they did not have enough evidence to charge you with a criminal violation. Unfortunately, that is not the case anymore. While we can all agree that you and Simon aren't fifty-fifty owners of BA Services and Jan and Sanjay raised the capital and sold the subscriptions, they do know that you own three percent of the company and Simon owns one percent. Furthermore, using a warrant, they went through the data on the computers and papers they confiscated from your office and know that you managed the team creating fake accounts and writing reviews and participated in those activities yourselves. They will charge you with fraud if you don't accept the deal, which will cost you much more in lawyer fees than the settlement they have offered. They also promised to work with your victims to facilitate civil lawsuits. Settling will be a much cheaper and quieter way of resolving this. To tell you the truth, I do think we could beat the criminal charges in court, since it isn't clear that posting fake reviews to Yauzzers is a crime. But I do think you could lose in court if those companies you posted bad reviews for started suing you. Even if you won those cases, the cost of defending yourselves would be astronomical."

This shut us both up while we let it all sink in. Neither of us even touched our drinks. Finally, I said, "Is that all? I mean the $10,000 fine. Keeping off of social media and review sites, and giving them any information they ask for?"

"Yes, though if they ever do capture Jan or Sanjay, you would also be required to give testimony against them. They also won't assist your customers if they sue you, unless, of course, they are ordered to by a court."

"Ok, I'll take the deal. I just want this to be over with and don't want any possibility of going to jail," I said.

"I'm not so sure. It sounds like you are pushing me into a deal by threatening to take my money if I don't go along," Leo said.

"That is the reality of the situation you put yourself in," Mr. Johnson coolly replied.

Leo dropped his head down into his lap and said, "O Fuck me." Then after a few more minutes of getting clarifications on the consequences of not taking the deal, he agreed to take it. That was it then. First thing the next morning, we would all go back to the federal building and sign the agreement. Again, Leo and I both headed our separate ways without talking about what had happened.

The process of going over the immunity deal in detail and signing it took a few hours but otherwise went smoothly.

Leo and I were directed to show back up after lunch so we could give our testimony and help them understand the information they had confiscated from our offices, and other information they'd received from investors and customers of BA Services. After signing the papers, Mr. Johnson assured us that we did not need him to be present for the interviews, given that we now had immunity. We could contact him by phone if we had questions or issues with the process.

Leo and I were now ready to stop ignoring each other, so headed over to McDonald's for lunch. We scooted past the homeless person sleeping in front of the restaurant entrance, ordered our food, and made our way to a booth in the back. After a few quiet moments enjoying my cheeseburgers, Leo finally started with, "This fucking sucks. Between the lawyer bills and the fine, I've lost half my savings."

That surprised me since it meant he had twice as much savings as I had. I was going to have to pay what I owed to Mr. Johnson's office in monthly installments. "You're lucky you can pay it all now, I'm going to be paying this off for the next year or two. I better start looking for a new job or I'll lose my apartment. I only have rent money for another two months."

"I'm not fucking lucky. I thought I would get rich, and now I owe three times more than I ever made at that fucking company," Leo angrily stated.

"You and me both. Jan and Sanjay played us. I would like to fucking beat their heads in with a baseball bat." I then ruminated on that thought for a few seconds, which actually made me feel better for the first time in days. Leo keyed into what I was thinking and started to feel a little better too.

"Well, that's never going to happen. They're probably back in India living it up on all the money they stole."

We finished our burgers and fries and headed back to the Federal building, hoping to get all this over with as soon as possible. Back in our now familiar interrogation room, Agents Darry and McMullen sat across from us. They looked pissed. Agent Darry started with, "Well, I guess you got off easy."

Leo, upset himself, quickly replied, "That's bullshit."

The Agents just ignored the comment and started with their questioning. The session lasted for over five hours. Our lawyer was right in that we knew more than we thought we knew. We weren't present when Jan and Sanjay pitched to investors or made sales calls to customers, but from what communication we did have with them, we had a pretty good idea of how those meetings went. We just had to be led in the right direction to jar our memories. We also detailed how RevGen went from a computer-powered service to a human-powered service.

When we got to the point of the conversation on how we had developed the reviews we wrote, it got a little awkward. They thought there must have been some formula we were following to maximize the effectiveness of each review we wrote. In the beginning, we did have basic heuristics on how to write the new reviews and did some quality control. As the workload increased and the staff and pay did not, we stopped caring and just put out a lot of crap. We were lower than trolls since we didn't even have a purpose. Some of the reviews they asked about didn't even make sense. For example, one review described how a 'customer's' chicken sandwich was covered in fly poop. I eventually just told Agents Darry and McMullen that by the end, we just didn't care anymore and were being silly. McMullen let me know unequivocally that I was a disgusting human being.

Leo and I also learned a lot from the two Agents, the first being that Magnum was really Jan. Magnum was paid $100,000, but it was really just money from the company going into Jan's personal account. It turns out there were other fake employees earning large salaries that we didn't know about. These pretend people did really well, compared to myself, who made less than $10,000 after subtracting all of the food and beer I'd bought without ever getting reimbursed. I would have made four times that much if I'd stayed at my IT job. Unlike us, they also knew Jan and Sanjay's last names, when they left the country, and where they were currently located in India.

Unfortunately, they were out of reach of the strong arm of the law, unless they were dumb enough to come back to the US. Sanjay's father was a powerful politician, so India was not going to send them back for allegedly committing a white-collar crime in the US. Jan, Sanjay, and the money were all gone. Only Leo and I were left to pick up the pieces. Given that no real justice was forthcoming, after we left the Federal building, we were done with our part, and the case was likely put on the shelf. Fortunately for me, the company I'd previously worked for was having a lot of trouble hiring and keeping good employees, so when I asked for my old job back, they gave it to me. I was no longer interested in trying to get rich by joining a startup.

Leo, on the other hand, wasn't done with startups yet. It turned out that our experience working at BA Services made us very attractive candidates for other startup companies. It didn't matter that we'd failed spectacularly and were charged with a crime. It just mattered that we weren't felons and had startup experience. Leo tried to get me to join another company with him, where they offered us both 1000 stock options and a decent salary, plus healthcare. I said no. Two years later, the company went public. Leo's options were worth half a million dollars one year after that.

# OLD AGE

It was a typical August day in Southern Arizona. The mid-afternoon temperature was 105 degrees and there wasn't a cloud in the sky. I was sitting outside in my plastic lawn chair with a beer in one hand and a beer in my other hand. Crap, I guess I'd opened a second beer without realizing I'd barely finished my first. That kind of thing was happening to me more and more often. Since moving to a little ranch-style house in Yuma two years before, I'd really let myself go. The previous weekend, a boy scout in town offered to help me across the street. I looked at him a little shocked and said, "How old do you think I am that I need help crossing the street?" He guessed 82. Being only 67, that should have been a wake-up call. It was not that I didn't care, it was just that I'd made a decision to enjoy the rest of my life by only making the easy choices, and I was sticking with that plan to the end.

I'd mostly stopped cooking for myself, so ate Mexican, fast food, or an occasional frozen pizza when I didn't feel like going out. My one aberration from the easy plan is that I went out to eat instead of getting deliveries. It kept me in contact with the community. I would like more variety, but those are the two most prevalent restaurant types by far in the area. Maybe I'd cook myself up a cold bowl of cereal some mornings if I didn't feel nauseous. I drank a lot of beer, which kept my stomach full, so I didn't overeat. When I left Seattle two years before, I weighed 130 pounds, but by now I was up to 205. My skin was fat and wrinkly from sitting outside in my shorts most days and probably why I'd aged in appearance so quickly. On the plus side, I had a killer tan. The neighbor kid made fun of me sometimes, since my front side was twice as dark as my backside. It didn't feel good to lie on my belly to even out the tan, and doing something that didn't feel good went against my easy-choice plan.

Even though I felt like crap every morning when I woke up, and my actual crap toggled from too soft to too hard daily, I was much happier on the easy plan. Junk food is tasty and makes me happy, and I probably couldn't stop eating it now if I wanted to. They say that junk food inflames the body and makes you depressed, but I was mildly depressed before letting myself go, so in my case, it improved things. The trick is to always have something ready to eat, like a pop tart, when you start to feel down. My VA benefits ensured that I could get all of the statins, metformin, beta-blockers, and other medications I needed to keep me upright for years to come. By upright, I just mean alive, since standing upright was starting to get more difficult. I may have needed to add another adjustment to the easy plan and go for a walk while that was still possible.

Next door to my house lived twin middle schoolers, Jenny and Kenny. Both of their parents worked long hours, so they were home alone all afternoon. Their mom worked at the local Walmart and their dad at a farming supply center. There were no other kids in our sparsely populated neighborhood, so they liked to come over and visit me when I was sitting in my lawn chair. I also shared my snacks with them, which I felt a little guilty about, but it made them happy, and they were good company. Their parents never complained, so I think they might have been glad to have someone watching over their kids during the day. Jan (their mom) gave me her cell phone number and said I should call if there was a problem. One time, Jan offered to bring me over some home-cooked food, which I thanked her profusely for, but ultimately had to decline. It had really gotten to the point where junk food was all I craved. To her credit, she didn't judge me or get offended. She did occasionally hint that I should take better care of myself, but I can't fault her for caring. If I died of a heart attack, her kids would have lost a friend and free babysitter. Maybe I was being too cynical, Jan was a very nice person.

Despite the heat, it really was a very nice day. There was a slight southerly breeze blowing toward the dairy farm a couple of miles north of me. The biggest downside of my location was that the air smelled like manure and fertilizer most days, but not when the wind came from the South. For all the bad smells I'd experienced in the city, the rural areas were where the real stink was.

My ten-year-old cat Jake was fast asleep on my aluminum lawn chair. I adopted him two days after moving to Yuma and you can say he was my inspiration for the easy plan. All Jake did was eat, crap, and sleep with occasional breaks in the routine to get a good stretch in. The biggest difference between Jake and me was that Jake got his food brought to him, while I still made the effort to go out. The lifestyle was more agreeable to him than me; however, while I was obese with withering skin, he was fairly lean and had perfect shiny dark gray hair.

It was 3:30 PM and I saw the school bus dropping off Jenny and Kenny. After they had dropped off their bags, they would come on over to hang out and eat snacks. This was my cue to shimmy off the chair and head back into the kitchen. My cabinets were well stocked, so it was just a matter of choosing correctly. We'd been eating lots of pop tarts, so I pushed past them to consider the cookies. There were so many good choices, but I focused on a colorful box of little round, cream filled, chocolate snack cakes I'd forgotten I even had. They were a couple of weeks past their sell-by date, but I think these things probably take decades to spoil. I paired the little round cakes with some lemonade.

As predicted, I could see the kids running over just as I was placing the treats on the porch table. They were normally well-mannered kids, but they didn't even acknowledge me before digging into their cakes and drinks. Kenny was about to grab his third snack cake, before I put a stop to his binge. Jan gave me a lot of leeway when it came to her children, but I didn't want to send them back sick. I just ate a single cake and already had a stomachache, which is saying a lot given how much garbage I put into my intestines; it tasted so good though. I made him go inside and make some buttered toast for the three of us, to finish filling the gaps in our stomachs.

Later, we settled down and Kenny said, "I've never had those before. My Mom can't even make cake that good."

"This is very important Kenny; you must never tell your mom that you like store bought snack cakes better

200

than her homemade cake." Even if it were true, this could hurt his mom's feelings, and I didn't necessarily want Jan to know I'd been feeding her kids processed snack cakes. They somehow seemed worse than pop-tarts or cookies.

"I might let it slip," Jenny chimed in.

"Nobody likes a tattletale, Jenny," I chided.

For the next ten minutes, we sat there in silence, just looking out at the tanned landscape. Usually, the kids couldn't stop talking, so I was worried I'd made them sick or finally pushed them to diabetes. "Are you guys okay? Nobody is talking!"

"Kenny came in last in gym class today and all the other kids are making fun of him," Jenny said. "They're teasing me about it too, and I didn't even have gym class today."

"Kenny, what was it you were last in?"

Before Kenny could open his mouth, Jenny interjected, "Everybody in class had to race around the track, and Kenny couldn't even make it all the way."

"Please let Kenny answer," I gently chided Jenny.

"There is nothing else to say. I couldn't run one lap around the track. I fell down halfway and thought I would start puking. Pete and Bruce made fun of me in the locker room. They wouldn't give me my pants until Mr. Kent came in. He saw them making fun of me, and they didn't even get in trouble," Kenny unburdened himself.

"I didn't know they stole your pants," Jenny chimed in gleefully.

"Okay, okay, don't tease your brother. Let's figure out how to solve this problem."

"What do you mean by that?" Kenny said angrily.

201

"I mean, you couldn't run around the track because you are out of shape and eat lots of junk food, so we can fix both of those problems."

They both simultaneously gave me sour looks and Kenny said, "You are the one that gives me all the junk food. It's your fault!"

"Pointing fingers won't get you around that track. Did you know that I used to be an ultramarathoner?"

"What is that?" they both asked at once.

"You know what a marathon is?"

"Yes, Uncle Jack runs them. It is a 26.2-mile race," Jenny correctly stated.

Impressed, I went on, "Exactly right! An ultramarathon is a footrace that is longer than a marathon. When I was in high school, I ran forty miles and even created my own race."

They looked at me wide-eyed with partially open mouths. Finally, Jenny couldn't contain herself any longer and started laughing. Kenny held it together, trying to remain respectful to his elder.

"What's so funny?"

"You can barely walk across a room, so how can you run forty miles?" Jenny questioned.

"I wasn't always old. Before I moved to Yuma, I was in good shape."

"I remember when you first moved in, you weren't fat yet," Kenny helpfully interjected.

"Exactly, before moving here I was in great shape."

"Why are you making yourself fat? Daddy says you lost pride in yourself," Jenny said.

I had to quickly suppress my anger. I didn't like Dave (their dad) judging me, and maybe the comment hit too close to home. "I didn't lose pride in myself, I just like junk food," I lamely responded. "But that's not the point. The point is that I can help you be the best runner in your school."

"How are you going to do that?"

"Instead of coming over here every day to eat sweets and sit with me, we're going to run."

Jenny looked at me dubiously and said, "How are you going to run?"

"Don't you worry about that. We'll start off slowly and build up to more and more distance over time."

"Yeah, real slow. Kenny can't run halfway around the school track, and you can barely lift yourself off your chair." Jenny was too smart for her own good.

"You talk big, but let's see you run with us. Starting tomorrow, be ready with your sneakers on and shoes tied."

"Why wouldn't we tie our shoes?"

"It's just an expression, Jenny, be ready to run tomorrow after school," I stated, somewhat frustrated.

"Fine, can we have more snack cakes?"

"No, we start getting in shape right now, and if I get you sick, your mom will be angry with me."

To keep my promise and run with Jenny and Kenny, I had to change my ways too. I did not have any real food in my house, so for the first time in as long as I could remember, I went out and ate something healthy. I went to the diner and got myself grilled chicken, a side salad with just vinegar on top, and a glass of water. I asked the waitress to leave out the potatoes that usually came with the dish. After dinner, I went to the grocery store and stocked up on eggs, chicken, vegetables, and other fresh, healthy items. For the first time in a while, I actually had a purpose and was excited by something other than when I could enjoy my next cheeseburger. I was excited about the next day and fell asleep happy and content.

I woke up the next day feeling like I had the flu. The first thing I did, after rolling out of bed, was to hurl in the toilet. It didn't make me feel better though. I was in a cold sweat and had the shakes. My mind and body were craving sugar and chemicals. I still had plenty of that in my cabinets, but I did my best to resist the urge to give in. I lasted five minutes before running into the kitchen and downing a blueberry pop tart. I felt better, but I also felt ravaged, like I'd just put my body through some unholy torture. I lay down on my couch, contemplating my life choices up until that point.

Going cold turkey was not going to work for me. I had to slowly ease myself off junk food. Whenever I felt myself going into withdrawal, I would eat a small treat to get me through it. I decided to put off going cold turkey until the next week, if I made it that far. I managed to get myself through most of the day with just a couple of cookies and half a can of beer. I could only get one broccoli floret down without feeling nauseous.

I was so caught up in my withdrawal that I'd lost track of everything else I was supposed to do that day. In the afternoon, I walked back out of my house after the tenth time going to the bathroom. Jenny and Kenny were staring at me as I hobbled out the door with my water bottle in tow.

"You look really bad," Jenny said, stating the obvious.

"I'm trying to get healthy so I can run with you guys," I weakly replied.

"You don't look healthy," Jenny said.

"This is what happens when you only eat junk food and beer and try to stop. I don't think I can run with you today, but we can still get started."

"Can I have another snack cake first?" Kenny asked expectantly.

"We're done with junk food. If you want to run around the track, you can only eat healthy food from now on," I snapped back.

"This sucks!"

"Watch your mouth, kid. Now, I promise by next week I'll be able to run with you, but for now, if I try to run, I'll drop dead. Let's start with jumping jacks. I'll count off."

For the next half hour, I had them do some simple exercises, like jumping jacks, push-ups, and sit-ups. My Army experience was going to come in handy for this mission. I wasn't going to scream at them and call them ladies, however. They both did great, so after they'd finished, I had them go inside to get some water. A few minutes later, they came back outside with crumbs on their shirts and guilty looks on their faces, so I knew they'd got into my cookie stash. I didn't say anything but knew I would have to clear all that crap out of my house after I finished going through withdrawal. At least they were not stealing my beer.

Five days after exiting the easy plan, the sugar and carb withdrawal symptoms finally started to dissipate. It was Monday morning and the second day in a row I didn't wake up nauseous and in a cold sweat. I had managed to go forty-eight hours without any alcohol or junk food to ease my symptoms. This also meant we would start running that afternoon, which would induce a new level of pain and sickness in my body until I got back in shape. At my age, getting back in shape would take months. The silver lining was that Kenny was in bad shape too, so we would go through this together, but at his age, he'd be running circles around me in short order.

To celebrate my new sobriety, I cleaned out all sweets and junk food from my kitchen and threw away my medication now that I didn't need it to counterbalance my bad habits. After cleaning up, I went back outside to sit in my chair as usual, only now I wore a hat and moved my chair over to a shady spot to avoid getting sunburned. Jake was sleeping in the lawn chair as usual. After much discussion, we mutually agreed that Jake would stay on the easy plan. He apparently had too much on his plate to go through a lifestyle change at this time.

At 3:30, I saw the school bus drop Kenny and Jenny off and got myself ready to go by doing a few twirls with my hips. Other than some cracking and popping noises, things were off to a good start, and I was ready to go. I looked over at Jake for support, but he was busy sunning himself. As soon as they came over, I told them to go inside, drink some water, and then be ready to head out on our first run. Five full minutes after I'd sent them in, they came back out with disappointed looks on their faces. "Is something wrong?"

Jenny cut to the chase and said, "Where is all of the food? We're hungry."

"There are apples in the fridge," I mentioned.

Both kids stood there for a while, mouths downturned, noses curled up, looking like they might start crying, but eventually, Jenny just said, "Whatever."

With that out of the way, we were ready to get going. My goal was to just run down the block and back, which was around half a mile. When we got to the turn-around point, I felt so good, I decided to just keep going. The kids were also keeping up, though Kenny looked miserable. Jenny just looked angry; she wasn't the kind to show weakness. My new plan was to run once around our block, which was about a mile in distance. To Kenny's credit, he made it around halfway through the loop before collapsing. For comparison, this meant he ran four times farther than his attempt to run around the school track.

"Come on Kenny, get up, you can do it," Jenny whined. Her words were encouraging, but her tone of voice was scolding.

"Just let him rest for a second and then we'll continue."

"I can't do it," Kenny said, looking up at me with wet eyes. Jenny just looked down on him with crossed arms, exasperated.

"Okay, we already ran as far as I was planning on. Get up and let's walk back the rest of the way. If you don't get up, you'll stiffen up," I said. What was also happening was that I was starting to stiffen up and worried that if I didn't get home soon, I wouldn't make it.

"Fine," Kenny complained, and then got up and started walking. Fifteen minutes later we were back on my porch. Jake was still holding fort in the lawn chair. Kenny collapsed again and was lying on my porch. Jenny didn't look worse for wear at all. I was suffering but determined to keep up a strong front until the kids left. Fortunately, ten minutes later, Jan was calling for the kids to come home. She must have gotten out of work early. I let them know how good a job they had done, and collapsed into my chair as soon as they were off my property.

The next thing I remember was opening my eyes and seeing darkness. I must have fallen asleep. Jake was up and scratching on the door, wanting his dinner. When I got my senses back, I realized how terrible I felt. I don't think I felt that bad when I was running actual ultramarathons. Every muscle in my body was fatigued. My first attempt to get off the chair was a failure; I got dizzy and fell back into it. With all of my effort, I finally made it back into the house and dumped some dry food into Jake's bowl. Then I just got into bed, quickly falling back asleep.

The next morning, I woke up with a slightly clearer head, but I had stiffened up to the point where it took me several minutes to get out of bed. By the time I made it to the toilet, I was seconds away from peeing myself. I was in no condition to cook a good meal; I wished I still had some of my snacks. Instead, I mixed some salt into a glass of water and drank it. After a few moments, that gave me the energy I needed to make some eggs and toast. I then got back in bed and took a long nap.

Jenny and Kenny were at my door as usual at 3:30 PM and ready to go. Unfortunately, I could still barely walk, but I had to try, since if I quit, Kenny probably would too. I tried to change the strategy. "One way to get in shape is to do something called run walking, where you walk a little and then run a little and keep switching. Since we're all feeling really tired from yesterday's run, let's try that."

"We're not tired," Jenny stated, seeing through my deception.

"I'm still sore from yesterday," Kenny said.

"Okay, the truth is that I'm sore too and I can't run around the block without walking part of it. So, Jenny, you can run the whole way if you want, but I'm going to start walking and then try to run a little after I loosen up," I said. Jenny pursed her lips and snorted out a deep breath, but just said, "Fine." Kenny looked relieved.

All three of us started walking at a very slow pace, which was dictated by the maximum speed my legs would move. About a quarter of a mile in, I started to loosen up and moved into a jog. Jenny used this as an opportunity to start running at her own pace and quickly left us behind. Kenny and I stayed with my plan and alternated between running and walking the rest of the way back, where Jenny was waiting for us on my porch eating an apple.

"Why are you two so slow?" she teased.

"I'm not slow," Kenny replied falsely.

"I've been sitting here for hours, you are slow."

They fought for a few more minutes, while I ignored them, not having the energy to intervene. Finally, I asked Jenny to go in and get us a couple more apples and water. That ended the arguing and the food improved Kenny's mood.

"Getting in shape is really hard at first, but trust me, in a few weeks, getting around the block will seem easy," I said.

"It already is easy," Jenny replied.

"For you, but Kenny and I are not fit, so it's going to take us longer."

"No kidding," Jenny said.

A few weeks later, it was easy for Kenny to run one mile around the block, but while Kenny and I were doing one lap, Jenny was doing three. After a few more weeks, I could do two laps, while Jenny was doing four. Kenny stuck with his one lap since he'd met his goal of being in shape enough to not get embarrassed in gym class. He hated sports and exercise, so I couldn't get him to do more. Jenny, on the other hand, had tons of energy and really liked running.

Two months later, I was running the first three laps with Jenny and then following her on the electric bike I bought to keep pace with her the rest of the way. As soon as she freed herself from my pathetic pace, she doubled her speed and was now up to running five miles a day. I'd also lost twenty-five pounds, with only around forty more pounds to go. Kenny was still running his one mile a day but managed it in just seven minutes. The kids in school were still teasing him about collapsing on the track, though. He would have to do a lot more than he was willing to do to erase that stain from his resume.

# THE RACE

Jenny continued to run with me through the end of eighth grade and into the summer. After school started back up, she joined the cross-country team. She was only a freshman in high school but had already won two out of her first eight cross-country meets. She was in the top five in the other meets, except her very first one, where she was uncharacteristically very nervous. Finishing at the back of the pack just made her angry, which fueled her to always get out in front from then on. Jenny and Jan both convinced me to volunteer as a coach over dinner at their house one night (now that I was off the easy plan, I could eat Jan's homemade cooking). The high school's longtime track coach had retired, and I was the only one of the three volunteers to coach track, who had experience running a long-distance race. When we met over coffee before the first practice, they volunteered me to act as the head coach. It was also a benefit that the head coaching job took a lot of time, and I was the only one of the three with nothing else to do (in their view anyway).

It had been over a year since I started running again and I was running around forty miles a week. I didn't bother trying to run with the kids, since I was much too slow. The slowest runners on the team ran seven-minute miles during the long runs and closer to six on race day. My pace was closer to twelve minutes a mile. Jenny was the fastest runner on the team and ran the 5K in just over fifteen minutes.

I didn't have a coaching method, so I just used what I knew from back when I was in high school. My approach was to just run as much as possible. We started practicing in mid-July and were now at the end of the season, and I already had them doing fifteen-mile runs once a week. I encouraged them to run even farther if they wanted. I liked to talk about my ultramarathon days to motivate them to work harder, but Jenny told me the other kids just rolled their eyes when I brought up the old days. I knew that already since I would occasionally hear an "Okay, Boomer," from the peanut gallery.

It was now late October, and I was coaching Jenny through her last meet of the season, the State Championship. Besides Jenny, three other boys and two girls from Yuma High School had made their way to Phoenix. Besides the kids, the other two coaches were present along with their families and the families of the six kids, plus a reporter from the local Yuma newspaper. This was a big deal.

The division three race was scheduled to start at 2:00 PM, so at 1:15 PM, I took the kids out for a leisurely warm-up run. 2:00 PM came and went, and our race was pushed back at least an hour, so I had them walk around in circles to keep them from tightening up. By 3:00 PM, their heat of forty-five kids was off and running. Jenny, as usual, got out in front of the girls quickly, but since the boys and girls were competing in the same race, she couldn't get out in front of all the racers, which led her to get crowded in with a bunch of boys. About halfway through the race, four other girls managed to pass her, and she finished fifth overall. That was a great result for a freshman, but Jenny was upset about getting caught in a tight pack of runners at the start of the race, which had significantly slowed her down.

We had nothing left to do after the race was over, so the whole Yuma contingent went out for some Mexican food before heading back home. All six of the runners finished in the top half of their categories, so we had a lot to celebrate. The parents paid for the coaches' food and drinks, so for the first time since I'd left the easy plan, I ate greasy food and drank alcohol; neon blue margaritas specifically.

It was all going so well, and then I felt a slight pain in the left side of my chest. I didn't want to spoil the mood, so I tried to ignore it. I stopped eating and just smiled and nodded my head while the others celebrated. At some point, I must have spaced out, since Dave looked at me and asked, "Are you alright?" I wasn't alright, the pain was shooting through my chest and down my arms and I could no longer breathe well enough to talk. I just put my hand to my chest and shook my head no.

One of the other moms in the group was a nurse and immediately took over, telling her husband to call 911. That was the last thing I remembered before waking up in a hospital bed hooked up to all kinds of tubes and beeping machines. I was having déjà vu. I was in a room with other patients and nurses and doctors walking around checking on this and that. One nurse saw I was awake and immediately called a doctor over to check on me.

214

I asked him what had happened, but he ignored me for a few seconds while checking over my vitals. He then said, "You had a heart attack, Mr. Zane. Fortunately for you, you got help quickly. Another few minutes and you might have had serious brain damage, though we still need to test that. We were able to revive you, obviously," he giggled, "and administered a few stents to open back up your arteries. You'll notice some soreness and bruising on your arm where we went in with the catheter."

This doctor's bedside manner needed work, since I immediately focused on one thing that he had said. "I have brain damage?"

"Probably not, but when you arrived, your heart was not beating. I think you'll be fine. Well at least fine for someone who's just had a heart attack," the Doctor joked. He then started to squeeze my ankles.

I wanted to change the subject. "How long have I been here?"

He looked at some papers by my feet and said, "You came in at 4:30 PM and it is now 9:00 PM, so four and a half hours. You hang tight now. It's perfectly normal for a 68-year-old to have a heart attack."

"Why is it normal? Was it the Mexican food I was eating before the heart attack?"

"No, no, the plaque's been building up in your arteries a lot longer than that. A lot of people your age have the same problem, so you're not special. You need to get some rest now," he replied.

He was then off to the next patient. "What the fuck?" Did he really say having a heart attack was perfectly normal? Maybe in his own way he thought he was comforting me.

I spent the rest of the night in the ICU, so I got very little rest with nurses and techs poking and prodding me all night. They decided I had recovered enough to move me to my own room in the morning, so it was a little quieter, but not much. I was still covered with monitors and was checked on and had blood drawn frequently. They did let Jan, Dave, Jenny, and Kenny come in to visit me, which was nice, though embarrassing.

"How are you doing? You gave us all a big scare," Dave said.

"I'm fine. Hopefully, they'll let me out soon," I said. I didn't know if I was fine or that I would go home soon, but it's what you say.

"Why did you have a heart attack?" Kenny said, cutting to the crux of the matter.

"Kenny, Simon didn't want to have a heart attack," Jan informed him.

"I know, Mom, but what did the doctors say?" Kenny replied.

I let Jan know that the question was okay and replied, "I have plaque in my artery near my heart, and that blocked the blood from flowing through. The doctors opened it back up and I should be as good as new."

Jenny interjected, "Why do you have plaque in your arteries?"

"It's all the junk food I ate."

Jan told the kids that was enough with the questions about my heart attack, but I could see from Kenny's

216

furrowed brows and pursed lips that he was confused. I said, "Are you okay, buddy?"

"When you had all the good food in your house and just sat around and drank, you were perfectly fine. Then you started exercising and eating apples for snacks and you got plaque. You should go back to eating like you used to," Kenny confidently stated.

"It doesn't work like that. We can talk more about it later," Dave chimed in to end the conversation. They all wished me well and left a balloon and a nice card behind, but they had to get back to Yuma. I wanted to be alone anyway; at least as alone as I could get with all the medical staff around. They were strangers, though.

Later that afternoon, they hooked my equipment up to an IV pole and made me walk up and down the hallway. For the next few days, they walked me four or five times a day, between feedings and bloodlettings. Finally, on day four, a nutritionist came to see me and put me on a low-salt and low-fat diet. The nurse spent half an hour going over my new prescriptions and discharge instructions. If I felt any more chest pain, they told me to check into the VA hospital in Yuma.

My car was still parked at the location of the cross-country meet, so I caught an Uber back to my car and made the three-hour drive home. Right before walking in the door, I had a sudden fear that I would find my cat dead; starved to death. Fortunately, the neighbors had thought of Jake and had cleaned up his litter and kept him fed. I let him out to sleep on the lawn chair and then took a seat myself, and just stared into space, contemplating life.

217

Sometime later, I woke up to someone tapping on my shoulder. Jenny and Kenny were standing over me. "Whoo, I thought you were dead," Jenny said.

"Not yet, you guys ready to go for a run?" I deadpanned.

They looked at me a little weird before I said, "Just kidding."

"I thought so, you look really pale. Do you feel okay?"

"He said in the hospital that he was just fine, Jenny, so stop bothering him," Kenny said angrily. They argued for a few seconds before I assured them both that I just needed to rest a while and then would be as good as new. Jenny looked unconvinced, being too smart to fall for my bull.

"Did you check your cabinet?" Kenny asked.

"No, what's in my cabinet?"

Kenny ran into my house and came out with a colorful box of cream filled chocolate snack cakes. "I think you need to get back to eating like you used to so this doesn't happen again." Kenny's advice would probably be the death of me, but he was very sweet for trying to cure me in a way that made sense to him.

Jenny grabbed the box out of Kenny's hands and told him in a tight voice, "Don't you understand, dummy, this is why he had a heart attack."

Giving it right back to her, he replied, "He didn't get a heart attack until he stopped eating snack cakes."

I liked seeing them, but I needed to rest in quiet, so I told them they were both right, but asked Kenny to put them back in the cabinet and then go home so I could take a nap. They agreed that I looked like I needed a nap, so they both gave me hugs and skipped back home.

In truth, they were both right. I had to spend some time going over the pluses and minuses of getting back on the easy plan. My original motivation for getting back in shape was to help Kenny run around the school track. He could do that now, and Jenny was on her way to becoming a champion cross-country runner. With my job done (well done), it might be time to get back on the easy plan. If I was going to die, then I should get to spend my last days eating junk food. The problem was, I didn't know if I would die soon or live for many years to come. I decided to go with pessimism and assume imminent death, which freed me to put chocolate snack cakes and ice cream back on the menu.

# END GAME

The next morning, I got up feeling pretty good. I looked through my fridge and cabinets and couldn't find anything I wanted to eat, so I headed out to a diner to get a stack of pancakes covered with syrup. I had made my choice and was back on the easy plan. The pancakes were good, but it had been so long since I'd indulged in this much sugar that I felt a little dizzy. I pressed on and managed to finish the stack of three large pancakes and a large orange drink they claimed was made from the juice of an orange. I left a big tip and quickly stood up, ready to face the day. I then, just as quickly, fell back into my chair as the head rush hit. I also had a moment where I couldn't catch my breath. A guy at the table next to me noticed and asked me if I needed help. I caught my breath and said I was fine; he just nodded and got back to nursing his coffee. I tried again, much slower this time, and successfully got to my feet and made it out of the restaurant.

The first order of business was to restock my kitchen. I had no more use for fruit, vegetables, and lean protein. Before I did that, I decided to drive to the park and take a walk. Even though a walk violated the easy plan, it was a nice cool sunny day and despite almost fainting at the diner, I felt pretty good for someone who had just had a heart attack. I put in my earbuds and started listening to a podcast. They were interviewing a movie star on SmartLess. As I passed by a small pond, a row of ducks was crossing the path ahead. Mom was in front, and all the ducklings dutifully followed behind. I held back until they were all safely off the path and onto the grass surrounding the pond; relieved that they were safe and sound, I continued.

After only around five minutes of walking, I realized that I was overdoing it. I dropped onto a park bench, out of breath and clammy, and sat there for a full fifteen minutes before getting the energy up to walk back to my car. Finally, after making the five-minute walk back in ten minutes, I was just a street crossing away from the safety of my vehicle. My earphones went dead, and I thought maybe I'd forgotten to charge them. I started fiddling with my phone as I stepped off the curb. Then, a very brief moment of shock, and then nothing.

It was déjà vu all over again, again. I was back in a familiar place, surrounded by complete darkness but still aware of being. For a long time, I was in a panic, enveloped in darkness and not able to move or communicate. It was like I had been rolled up into a carpet and left to die in a dark closet. At least I think it was a long time; I had no sense of the passing of time. I may have been there for minutes or years for all I knew.

I could not physically feel or hear directly, but those senses were still active enough to leave me with dulled sensations of stimuli I might have been experiencing. I detected pressure on the body I was convinced I still had, but was no longer attached to my conscience. I sensed mumbling in the distance that I knew was distinct from my own thoughts and dreams. I was sure there were some people that would enjoy this. Maybe I was in a state that people who crave psychedelics are striving for. Maybe I would have enjoyed myself more if I could have just relaxed. I couldn't even lighten up in a coma.

I'd experienced something similar to this before, shortly after I started to chew on my Sergeant's arm. This was how I knew I was in a coma. Being in a coma also validated my choice to eat that stack of pancakes. I would be much more upset if my last meal had been a dried-out cut of chicken breast with a side of broccoli. I hoped Kenny at least got to enjoy the snack cakes he'd brought me.

After several more months, minutes, or decades, I don't know which, I started to get bored. I just was not interesting enough to entertain myself for all eternity. I used to pass the time by watching a lot of shows, so I decided to imagine watching the television. At first, this helped me to pass the time pretty well. I visualized myself sitting in front of a big screen with videos of talking heads debating sports and adventurous couples RVing around the country. Over time, my memories of videos and television shows I used to watch started to fade and my efforts to fabricate my own shows failed. In the end, I spent months, minutes, or decades, whatever, just staring at a fuzzy screen.

My next attempt at keeping my sanity was to start running again. Visualizing going for a run was effective. My brain cells had lots of experience running for hours on end, so I could almost feel like I really was running just by imagining it. I even had the sense of physical tiredness after a long run. Sometimes Jose and Matty would join me, and we would run along the Hudson River, joking about the old times. Between runs, I visualized eating Mexican food and cream filled chocolate cakes with Jenny and Kenny. I found my way back to the easy plan, despite being in a coma.

All in all, things were actually starting to look up. I was sitting on my porch, with Jake asleep in the lawn chair by my side. I was running ultramarathons again without any of the post-run aches and pains. I was living on junk food without any of the constipation or diarrhea. I pretended to spend my afternoons hanging out with the kids and even had a weekly Sunday dinner at their house, cooked by Jan.

I'd just finished a burrito when I noticed something was off. Why do bad things happen to me after eating Mexican food? I was about to visualize leaving the restaurant and driving home when the other people in the restaurant started to blink in and out. I looked up at the waitress's face, and it was just a black hole. Then I lost the ability to create any imagery and could only sense blackness. Then I started losing my thoughts. My last thought before I ceased to exist was "Why?"

# EPILOGUE

Doctor Jacobs was at his desk reviewing the patients in his care. Several months ago, a patient named Simon, with severe injuries, including a broken spine, skull, and many other blunt force trauma injuries, was dumped by the local hospital's ICU at the nursing home where Doctor Jacobs runs the medical department. His facility was not set up to care for coma patients and if he had not been on an extended vacation, he would never have allowed the hospital to dump Simon in his nursing home. This one patient took up a disproportionate chunk of his budget and the time of the nursing staff, who should have been caring for patients who weren't permanently horizontal yet. Unfortunately, Simon still showed brain activity so they couldn't bag him, and his efforts to get the hospital to take him back were tied up in the courts.

Doctor Jacobs had a plan though. That morning, the nurse who usually does the morning rounds was out sick, and given the limited staffing, Doctor Jacobs must occasionally substitute in to do the nursing rounds himself. He had been patiently waiting over a month for this scenario to unfold after coming up with his plan, and that morning, the stars finally aligned. A couple of weeks before, they had started adding some vitamin supplementation to Simon's IV bag to correct some imbalances that had shown up in his bloodwork. And on that fateful morning, Doctor Jacobs also added a very small amount of ricin to the mix.

He was a little worried about Simon getting suspicious symptoms that would result in questions being asked. He need not have worried. The next day, Simon passed quietly, and nobody questioned how it had happened. The pathologist did a cursory job and determined kidney failure as a probable cause, but since Simon also had end-stage heart failure, he could have listed that also. After months in care and the damage from his accident, Simon's kidney bloodwork showed concerning measurements, so the pathology results were no surprise.

As a side benefit, this ended the court battle between the nursing home and the hospital, which was a relief to all parties involved, except possibly the lawyers justifying their billing. Doctor Jacobs could take personal comfort in doing Simon and his staff this small mercy. All in all, he could go home at night, proud of his work, the care he provided his patients, and the kindness and professionalism he extended to his staff.

# Thank You

Thank you for reading *Simon's Run and Other Adventures* and I hope you enjoyed the book. Please help support *Simon's Run* by recommending it on social media or to a friend, and leaving a review, so I can hear your comments.

Please visit SaddWritings.com to find out more.